DINNER TIME

"We're stuck!"

The wheels of the Land Rover spun deeper and deeper into the soft mud of the riverbank.

"We need to stick a branch under the wheel," said Jonny.

"I'll help," said Jessie, jumping out of the four-by-four with Hadji and Jonny.

Together, the three of them dragged a big limb out of the bushes. They were just sticking it under the wheels when Jessie gasped.

"Over there, guys!"

Jonny turned. Slithering toward them were three huge crocodiles!

Their mouths gaping wide—

Read all of
The Real Adventures of Jonny Quest™
books

The Demon of the Deep
The Forbidden City of Luxor
The Pirates of Cyber Island *

by Brad Quentin

*coming soon

JONNY QUEST
THE REAL ADVENTURES

THE FORBIDDEN CITY OF LUXOR

BRAD QUENTIN

HarperPrism
An Imprint of HarperPaperbacks

This is a work of fiction. The characters, incidents, and
dialogues are products of the author's imagination and are not to
be construed as real. Any resemblance to actual events or persons,
living or dead, is entirely coincidental.

HarperPaperbacks *A Division of* HarperCollins*Publishers*
10 East 53rd Street, New York, N.Y. 10022

First printing: August 1996

Printed in the United States of America

HarperPaperbacks, HarperPrism and colophon are trademarks of
HarperCollins*Publishers*

❖ 10 9 8 7 6 5 4 3 2 1

To Nichols Silbersack

Note:
While Ranthambhore Preserve exists as described in this book, the cities and villages surrounding it, and the Forbidden City of Luxor are fictional.

1

DANGERS LURKED IN THE JUNGLE.

Everyone knew that. When you were born in a village like Jakphur in central India, you learned that quickly.

Ranjit had learned.

You learned about the huge fanged tigers and the coiling snakes and the clawed insects that could eat you alive. You learned about the sucking quicksand and the dense foliage. You learned how easy it was to get lost in the forest, swallowed up in the moist green mist.

Ranjit knew this as he made his way through the trees.

And yet he was curious. He had heard about wonders and new dangers, and he wanted to find out what they were.

If he were not a boy who had often gone into the jungle, perhaps he might not have been so brave. But his father had taken him frequently. Sometimes they hunted. Sometimes they just explored. It was good education for a young Indian boy. He learned much about the animals and the plants.

Now, though, he wanted to learn more of these new mysteries: the strange creatures people had reported, the lights . . .

Even though he lived in a village, a city was not far away. India was full of superstition, but it wasn't as though modernization of some kind hadn't been introduced. Ranjit could read, and he saw motion pictures and newspapers and television. He didn't really believe in ghosts or UFOs. His dearest wish was to make enough money so that he could go to a good school in New Delhi or Bombay and become an engineer. He was an excellent pupil in the local school, but the classes were so big and the teachers so few he had to puzzle out most of the work himself from torn old textbooks.

Perhaps he could somehow not merely satisfy his curiosity out here in the forest of the Ranthambhore Preserve. He could write a story for a national newspaper and make a lot of money—

Cheep!

Clatter!

Up in the trees there were squeakings and scurryings.

Ranjit jumped. But he calmed down right away.

He looked up to the jagged branches, etched black against the big ball of the almost full moon. Prancing and scrabbling there were a bunch of monkeys. Langur monkeys, by the look of them.

Ranjit smiled to himself.

The little mischievous devils. If they had their way, they'd be playing more elaborate tricks on humans. As

2

it was, they were just enjoying the forest shenanigans going on now.

The Indian jungle was full of monkeys. It was full of all kinds of plants and animals, in fact. India had perhaps the greatest variety of both in the world. But even a land with so much natural wealth was feeling the strain of the encroaching modern world. That was why areas such as this had been designated as wildlife preserves, places where endangered species could grow and replenish their numbers once more.

Species such as the tiger.

Ranjit felt a shiver of fear.

Tigers!

They certainly were out there, tigers. But Ranjit knew this land, and he knew this was not an area that tigers liked much, since so many humans came. Still, he'd seen them. They were magnificent creatures, the most efficient killing machines on earth.

But they didn't kill humans.

At least not often.

Another delicious shiver went through the boy, and he moved on through the forest.

The place smelled of damp and rot and danger. But it also smelled of the sweet exotic flowers that bloomed this time of year, and of the rich pulse of life. Ranjit knew the forest's beauty and its darkness.

Now he wanted to know the secret it held.

He pulled out an ancient Kodak camera from the pocket of his khaki pants. Whatever he found, he was going to get pictures of it for his news story.

He hurried on. From what people said, the lights

were best viewed from the other side of that hill over there. They sprang up from the middle of the night, over toward the huge lake in the middle of the preserve. They glittered like a god's eye, his old friend Khurum the rug vendor had told him. But Ranjit had been warned to stay away, because they could very well be the eye of a demon.

Ranjit found the rocky path. There was not so much vegetation here, for the path was well traveled not just by local villagers but by the tourists who came to gawk. Long ago, the foreigners had also come to shoot their guns . . . but no longer.

Rocks gave way under one of his sneakers. They tumbled down a cliff, clattering into a nest of vines.

However, Ranjit had climbed many hills—yes, even mountains—and had excellent balance. He righted himself, recovered, and was again on his way. This would not have happened to him during the day. It was harder to see bad footing by moonlight than it was in the clear, hot Indian day.

Up ahead, near that old tree . . . that was where they said the best viewing was. Over past the hills and out toward the silver glow of the lake.

Ranjit picked his way down over the mossy rocks and positioned himself, bracing his back against a boulder. He brought up the camera. He fiddled with the settings. Excitement played in his stomach like impatient moths.

Wow. Perfect view. All he needed was to be patient, to wait for the lights. He'd brought a container of *chai* if he got thirsty. And a pot of *dal* if he got hungry.

But if what everybody said was true, then he wouldn't have to wait long.

The trip had made his mouth dry. He pulled the *chai* out and unscrewed the top of the container. The sweet and milky tea tasted really good.

He closed his eyes, savoring its delicious spices.

When he opened his eyes, there was a goddess standing just yards from him.

No, not standing.

Floating.

Kali, the goddess of death. Her many arms flailed wildly, and the steely knives she held blazed against the dark of night. Her eyes were like pinpricks of sunfire, and they seemed to bore through Ranjit's very soul. The mouth of the creature opened, and a snarl flowed out.

The *chai* flew out of the boy's grasp, smashing and splashing against the rocks.

Kali started to come for him.

"Ranjit," she seemed to say in words made of piercing needles. "I hunger for you. Come to me!"

The Kodak camera dropped from the boy's hands, cracking as it hit a stone.

Ranjit turned and ran for his life.

2

HOLDING UP A SMALL CAMERA, JONNY QUEST STEPPED BACK, unaware of the snake.

"Hadji! Jessie! Smile!"

Suddenly Hadji called, "Hey, guy! Stop!" He held up his hand in warning.

"Jonny, watch out!" cried Jessie.

Jonny's reflexes were good. He stopped instantly and swiveled around.

Behind him in the bazaar was a dark-skinned man. Around his head was a turban, and wrapped around his midsection was a towel. In his hand was a handmade flute, and on his face was a look of extreme alarm.

In front of him was a basket from which a black snake rose. Jonny recognized the kind of snake instantly. A hood seemed to grow from either side of its head, and its eyes looked black and deadly. A long tongue slithered from its mouth.

A cobra!

"Yikes! Sorry," said Jonny. The blond-haired teenager's blue eyes went wide. Son of the famous

Dr. Benton Quest, he hated when he made mistakes like these—especially when he was in a foreign country. Jonny's dad was a perfectionist, and he expected perfection from his son as well.

Doctor Benton Quest was one of the world's foremost scientists and inventors. His insatiable curiosity had taken him out of the lab to explore the furthest reaches of the world. His goal: to solve the puzzles and mysteries of the planet earth. Now, he had a team to help him. The Quest Team. And Jonny Quest took great pride in being an *important* member of that team.

The Indian hastily picked up the wicker top of the basket and spoke comfortingly in Hindi to the snake.

The snake hissed and spat.

Jonny dodged and moved back another pace, bumping into Jessie.

"Feeling a little jet-lagged?" teased Jessie. Her father was Race Bannon, and she had his eyes, his jet-black hair, and his sense of humor as well. She was a year older than Jonny, but sometimes Jonny felt as though she were years older, years more sophisticated. She had such a tart, sardonic, *adult* sense of humor.

The snake charmer stepped slowly around the basket, still whispering in his native tongue. Then, swiftly, he recapped the basket and gave it a twist, trapping the venomous serpent.

Hadji went to the man, and they spoke for a moment while Jonny took out a handkerchief and mopped some of the sweat off his brow.

Jonny's father had informally adopted Hadji Bingh

when Hadji was young (he was two years older than Jonny), but the boy had been born in India and knew the languages and customs. Hadji was a muscular, good-looking lad with deep brown eyes. He wore a turban around his head, in honor of the customs of his people—and as a sign of his own dedication to the spiritual path of yogin.

"Hadji," Jonny said, "tell him I really apologize."

"I think rupees work better than words in these situations," said Jessie.

"Um, okay." Jonny felt really stupid. Halfway across the world, the last thing he wanted to do was to make a bad impression. He always felt, on these international jaunts, that he was a representative of the American people. The people looking on and muttering among themselves now probably thought all Americans were klutzes.

The snake charmer nodded. He looked at the money, then smiled and waved it away. He spoke quickly.

Hadji interpreted. "The man says, 'I am not a rich person. But your friend tells me you are here to help protect my people from the lights in the sky. Please, keep your money—but also please remember to be cautious of snakes in the jungle.'"

The man shrugged and smiled. He pointed at a pot on the ground and laughed. Then he spoke again.

"'However,'" Hadji translated, "'if you would like to offer something to the snake . . . '"

The crowd laughed.

Jonny smiled. "Yeah. Sure." He peeled off a note

8

and placed it in the pot. Almost immediately he was surrounded by the outthrust hands of beggars, old and young alike, eager for a handout. Their eyes gleamed in their brown faces.

Hadji waved at the beggars, spoke some words to them, and then pulled Jonny away. "Hurry, or they'll think we're the U.S. Treasury visiting."

Jessie followed.

So did the crowd.

"Hmmm. Looks like I've let the genie out of the bottle," said Jonny.

"Only this genie wants cash, not freedom," said Jessie.

Hadji turned, put his hands to his mouth, and shouted at the people following. They turned and fled.

"What did you say to them?"

"I told them you have American cyber-leprosy," said Hadji, grinning.

"What, he touches them and their hard drives rot?" asked Jessie with a smile.

"Well, whatever it was, it worked," said Jonny. "C'mon, let's go to a different part of the market. I'd like to look around a little more. And I promise not to run into any more snake baskets."

"Get all the goofs and gaffes out of your system now," said Hadji. "This is an important mission."

Jessie nodded. "I guess when Dad and Dr. Quest finish taking care of those details, we'll get the full story." While they'd brought some necessary equipment with them—Jonny's dad had scads of equipment from his other investigations—they still needed to arrange to borrow some additional items.

Right, thought Jonny. Adults *were* useful sometimes. They could do things such as rent vehicles and procure necessary equipment. He could hardly wait until he was old enough for a driver's license and credit cards.

While Dr. Quest and Jessie's father were off making final arrangements, Jonny, Jessie, and Hadji had the afternoon free, so they had decided to go out and see a little of the town.

"We're here to do our best," said Jonny. "And I, for one, mean to solve this puzzle of the mysterious lights and apparitions. But we've got a couple more hours to play tourist before the government official shows up to brief us on where this phenomenon is taking place. In the meantime, I want to take in some of the sights."

"When we are out in the jungle in the land of the tigers," said Hadji. "Let us hope that the sights don't take *us* in."

Jonny turned and snapped a couple of pictures. The place was absolutely *amazing.* It was the main market area of the town of Gutpa.

They'd arrived that morning on a prop plane out of Bombay International Airport after a long trip by jet from Dulles International. Jonny was thrilled at the opportunity to help solve the enigma of the lights. He knew his dad was proud of him, but it was nice to prove himself from time to time. Besides, eventually he and Jessie and Hadji were going to be old enough to take on challenges on their own, and Jonny figured it was best to get accustomed to that.

The bazaar was a pulsing display of bustle, exotic smells, and raucous sounds. Colors paraded everywhere—earth tones collided with bright oranges and reds. Vendors grilled vegetables in the open air. Jonny recognized the smell of ginger and cardamom, but there were many others in the mix he could not identify. Buyers bargained with vendors for clothing. A holy man in a robe sat on a colorful mat and sang a wailing song to the heavens. Parrots squawked in cages.

"It's all so timeless," said Jessie, looking about in amazement. "Hadji, what's that man selling over there?"

Hadji canted his ear. "Um . . . time-share condo vacations, Jessie."

"No way," said Jonny.

Hadji's face split into a grin. "Would you believe hundred-megahertz laptop computers with five-hundred-megabyte hard drives? No?" He shrugged. "I know much of India seems old-fashioned. But my people also have much that is modern and progress-seeking—"

"I'm not criticizing," said Jessie. "I think it's wonderful."

"Ah, what would be truly wonderful, Jessie," said Hadji with a wistful look on his face, "is if so many of my people were not so poor. It is a rich life here, yes. Always. But it is a hard life as well."

Jonny put a hand on his friend's shoulder. "I know

11

how you must feel, Hadj. You must be proud, though, of your heritage."

Hadji smiled again. "Heritage! Oh, yes. The history and culture of India—why, it is a panorama amazing beyond compare. Did I tell you that I once sat under the very same Bodhi tree where Buddha attained enlightenment? I meditated there!"

"Did you get any results?" said Jessie respectfully.

"Yes—a very sore rear end. The ground was quite hard." Hadji grinned. "Come. I believe I was told the vendor we want is over here."

The trio turned a corner.

Beside a brick-and-earthen building stood a stall. A large awning protected a number of books and pictures from the sun and any sudden rain. Standing at the stall was a man in shorts, a pith helmet, and a riding crop, leafing through a book. When he turned sideways to talk to the clerk, Jonny recognized him.

Jonny froze and stopped his companions. "Uh-oh," he said. "Guys, we've got a problem!"

3

"PROBLEM?" SAID HADJI. "WHAT PROBLEM?"

"What are you talking about, Jonny?" said Jessie.

"Let's just quietly go back around the corner and talk about this, okay, guys?" Jonny stepped around them, turned, and beckoned them to follow.

He ran smack into a man. "Oops! Sorry, I—" Then he saw who it was and had a second surprise.

"Blimey, if it isn't Jon Quest, Esquire," said a heavyset man with a London cockney accent. He was wearing a khaki suit with boots and a tie. He peered at them, his eyes enormous behind thick black horn-rimmed glasses. "Fancy meeting you here." His smile wasn't friendly at all. One of his front teeth was silver.

"Right. Yes, well, it's been great. Bye. C'mon, guys," said Jonny.

The man had his dark hair in a crew cut. He spread out long arms with hands the size of table-tennis paddles, blocking their way.

"Oh, no, no. You mustn't go, not before the guv'nor bids you his salutations." The man lifted his head and brayed, "Doctor! Oh, Doctor! Look 'oos 'ere, then!"

The man in the pith helmet turned. He slammed the book in his hand shut with a loud clap. Hands and riding crop behind him, he marched toward them.

When he reached them, he took a monocle from a pocket and fixed it over his right eye. He leaned forward slightly, apparently not knowing at first who the three teenagers were.

When he realized that Jonny was among them, the monocle popped from his eye with surprise.

"Well, well, well," he said in a clipped, upper-class British accent. "Heavens! If it isn't Dr. Quest's offspring. And associates! How very delightful. Jon, would you care to make introductions?"

"What are *you* doing here?" said Jonny. Any fear he felt was overcome by annoyance and indignation.

This *wasn't* a good man.

"You know, the problem with you people in the American colonies is that you've never mastered the concept of politeness." The man then turned to Jessie. "Good afternoon. My name is Dr. Benjamin Hyde-Pierce, late of St. Unwin's College, Cambridge, England."

"I'm Jessie."

"Charmed, I'm sure." The man took her hand and pressed his lips to it politely.

Then he turned to Hadji. "And you must be Hadji. I have heard so many glowing comments about your programming abilities."

"I thank you," said Hadji.

14

The man smiled, showing a large gap between his teeth. He had black hair that was slicked back with some sort of cream, glistening in the hot sun. He had a neat slash of a mustache and a dimple in his chin. He was perhaps a few years older than Dr. Quest.

"And this, my young friends, is my associate, Higgins Doodle. Higgins hates India, I'm afraid."

"'Lo, mates." Higgins Doodle tipped his hat. "Too hot for my taste. Makes a bloke irritable." The man gritted his teeth, and for a moment he looked more like the pirate Long John Silver than a friendly Londoner. "But I'm sure we'll get on famously."

"If we don't see you first," said Jonny, looking not at Doodle but directly into the British doctor's dark eyes. "I don't want to get into ancient history, but I'm wondering why you aren't in jail. We've got a file on you a yard long back at QuestWorld, though Dad never could prove you fouled up his exhibit at that conference."

"What file?" said Jessie.

Jonny nudged her to be quiet. "So I'm advising you that we're going to inform the local authorities of your presence. I'm going to warn them about you, Doctor . . . I can promise you that!"

"My goodness, Higgins," Hyde-Pierce said, addressing his associate. "Nothing like coming to what used to be the British Raj to be on the receiving end of good old-fashioned American hostility."

Doodle shrugged. "Whatever you say, guv'nor."

Hyde-Pierce turned to Jessie and Hadji. "Despite what your friend here says, we're quite respectable, I

15

assure you. I am an eminent scientist. My specialty is physics, and I am presently working on strange atmospheric phenomena. I hope to write both academic and popular books on the subject. It is only natural that the lights in the Ranthambhore Preserve would attract my attention. I presume that's what's brought the Quest Team here as well, hmmm? Investigation of these marvelous wonders? And where, pray tell, are the estimable Dr. Quest and his faithful dog, Race?"

"The dog's name," said Jessie through gritted teeth, "is Bandit. My father, who is Dr. Quest's assistant and bodyguard, is Race—Mr. Bannon to you."

"Ah. Another progeny," said Hyde-Pierce. "And a lovely one, too. Again, may I ask if your fathers are here?"

"They certainly are," said Jonny. "And I don't doubt that my father will make sure the authorities know you're here, Dr. Hyde-Pierce."

The British scientist leaned over, lights dancing in his dark eyes. "Perhaps we should bury any past . . . misunderstandings. And if Dr. Quest and his crony still hold a grudge, then perhaps the younger generation will desire peace. We can work together, exchange information. Now that would be a hands-across-the-water kind of example to the nasty, competitive world of science, what?"

"Not," said Jonny. "I'm sorry if I'm too honest for you, Doctor, but I don't see us working together. Sorry."

Hyde-Pierce stood back and smacked his hand with

16

his riding crop. Jessie and Hadji jumped, but Jonny stood firm.

The smile on Hyde-Pierce's face stiffened. "Well, then, so be it. However, if you should have a change of heart on the matter, please contact us at our hotel. Higgins, would you be so kind?"

The hefty man took out a card and handed it to Jessie. He winked.

"Now, good day," said Hyde-Pierce, tipping his pith helmet. "These two Englishmen, I'm afraid, must get out of the midday sun and partake of some tea. Farewell." The duo sauntered jauntily down the road and around the corner.

"Come on," said Jonny. "Let's get those books we need and then go to our meeting."

"Jonny, who *were* those men?" said Jessie.

"Trouble," said Jonny Quest. "With a capital *T*."

"I could do with a spot of tea, I could, guv'nor," said Higgins Doodle happily.

Benjamin Hyde-Pierce whacked his henchman on the arm. Doodle barely flinched. He just stopped walking and turned around, staring dumbly down at the doctor.

"You numskull. We're not going to have tea. Come back here!"

Blinking, Doodle followed his employer back past a fruit stall to the corner of a building. Together they peered around the corner.

"The good news, Higgins," said Hyde-Pierce, "is

that the Quest lad's foul father does not know we are here quite yet. Blast, I hate the fellow. The bad news is that when his son tells him, the Quest Team could very well cause some problems for our efforts here."

Doodle nodded. "Right. Too bad they won't cooperate, guv'nor. You want I should—er—eliminate the little buggers?" A greasy, dumb smile spread over the thug's big face.

"What? Snuff the light from those innocent children?" said Hyde-Pierce. "Harm those hopes for peace and joy in this troubled world?"

Higgins looked puzzled. "Right. I guess that was the general idea."

Hyde-Pierce shrugged. "That would solve some of our problems, I suppose. Follow them, Higgins, my boy, while I make some preparations in light of the Quest Team's presence. See what's up with them. Absorb. Collect data. They could have information that would be to our gain. However, that done, if the opportunity emerges . . ." The scientist slid a finger across his throat in a precise surgical stroke.

"THOSE GUYS ARE CAPABLE OF MURDER!" SAID JONNY.

Hadji almost spilled his *chai*.

"My leg you are pulling!" Hadji exclaimed, his Indian accent growing thicker with his shock.

Jonny sipped his *lassi,* a calming yogurt drink. "No. Dad says those guys may well be criminals. He just can't *prove* it."

"Too bad we can't reach your dad now," said Jessie. She cocked her head quizzically. "You're sure this isn't just scientific competition talking?"

"I don't know. Like I said, I wasn't at that conference in London. But it was those guys who had the most to gain from stealing that stuff—and the most opportunity."

"It is true—they do not look like innocent lambkins," said Hadji. "What is the movie term for someone like Mr. Doodle—tendon?"

"*Muscle,* Hadj," said Jonny. "He's got other skills and talents, too, believe me. He just seems a little dense, the way he talks."

Jessie shook her head and looked at her watch. "Well, whatever the case may be, we'll just have to keep an eye on them. I don't know—scientists are supposed to compare notes, aren't they? I mean, we're all after knowledge and understanding. That's why we're here." She looked around. "Where *is* this official we're supposed to meet?"

"With my dad, Race, and Bandit," said Jonny. "Bandit has to get those shots so he won't get sick. They'll be along in a moment."

"I only know that if I drink one more cup of *chai,* I'll be as wired as my laptop," said Hadji.

Jonny looked down at his drink. It was good, but he would have preferred a vanilla malted. He'd told them as much as he could about Benjamin Hyde-Pierce: how he'd been quietly removed from his professorship at Cambridge University for reasons that had been kept very hush-hush. Jonny could remember only some of the things his dad had said about Hyde-Pierce, but none of them were good. If only they'd been able to use their laptops to dial into Questworld's computers, they'd have all the info they needed right on their screens. But their equipment was in the hotel suite.

Oh, well, Jonny thought, *Jessie's right.* They needed to focus on the reason they'd come to India: the lights. All they needed was the guy who could show them around and tell them what was what.

They were in the Hotel Calcutta's lounge now, stretched out on plump, comfortable chairs. Fans above them gently stirred the air-conditioned air. The place smelled of fresh-cut flowers and should have been relaxing.

Jonny couldn't relax, though.

First, this kind of mission was a heavy responsibility. And the appearance of those two troublemakers, Hyde-Pierce and Doodle, sure didn't help. Now the guy who was supposed to be their contact was almost an hour late.

"Oh, dear," said a short man in a white suit and tie, rushing toward them from the hallway. "Hello, hello, Jonny Quest! Welcome to India. Welcome to—"

He tripped over a footrest and staggered toward them, arms windmilling. He fell face first, right beside their table. The briefcase he was carrying fell open, spilling papers and pictures everywhere.

"Hello!" said the man. "I am Kailish Thakpur, and goodness, do we have some strange phenomena for you!"

There had been some complications in getting Bandit's shots, Mr. Thakpur explained. Dr. Quest and Race would be along in a moment. In the meantime, he was supposed to fill them in on what was happening.

He did so.

"Lights, Mr. Thakpur?" said Jonny.

"Please, call me Kailish. Yes, lights. An amazing display of lights."

"What sort of lights?"

Kailish thumbed through the jumbled pile of papers

on the table before them. He'd picked himself up and ordered himself a cup of coffee, and Jonny, Jessie, and Hadji had helped him put things back into place, but the enthusiastic man still seemed flustered.

"All kinds of lights. Some look like laser lights, some like rainbows, and some like the aurora borealis," said Kailish.

"But the aurora borealis is found only near the magnetic north pole!" said Jessie.

"Aye. What's it doing in the middle of the Indian subcontinent? Good question. Ah. Here." He produced a glossy photograph. "This was taken by a man who happened to be in the right place with the right camera."

Jonny examined the photo. It showed a landscape filled with jungle and hills. Far away, multicolored lights twirled toward the sky like a rock-and-roll laser show.

"Heavens," said Jessie.

"The question is," said Hadji, studying the picture closely, "what are these lights doing in the middle of a nature preserve populated only by wildlife?"

The teens had bought a book about the preserve at the stall. Ranthambhore was a huge area of jungle, hills, plains, and lakes declared by the Indian government as a nature preserve in 1978. In India many species of animals were rapidly disappearing—most notably the Indian tiger. By giving the tiger and his brethren part of the country back, the government hoped these endangered species would survive.

To create the preserve, whole villages had had to be moved from the area. Currently no one was allowed in

22

Ranthambhore without official permission, least of all the hunters who had so decimated the tiger population over the centuries.

The scheme had worked, for the wildlife of Ranthambhore was thriving.

But what were lights like these doing coming from the very midst of it all?

"You think the tigers are having a hoedown?" said Jessie.

"That I should like to see!" said Hadji.

"Unfortunately, planes we have sent over the area have seen nothing," said Kailish. "Radiation detectors show nothing unusual. We have even looked at Landsat photos. Zero!" The man threw his hands up in the air. "There is no threat here, you see. No problem, really. Oh, the lights frighten people, certainly—but they do no damage. The ministry has therefore relegated it to a spot far down on the list of matters to be dealt with. I, on the other hand, am most fascinated. I think this could be very important for India . . . and possibly for the world." The dark face opened with a warm smile. "I have heard of your father's work. *Your* work, Jonny Quest. I thought this might be your cup of tea!"

Jonny nodded. "What about spectrometry?"

"Ah, yes," said Kailish. "Unfortunately, we've not been able to analyze the lights in person, as it were. But pictures like these have of course been pored over by our scientists. These lights seem to be not merely emanations but refractions of emanations. This is what causes their variety."

23

Jonny nodded. Kailish meant that the lights were neither directly projected into the air nor reflected off something like a mirror. Rather, the lights were being refracted—the beams of light were passing *through* something and getting bent or changed in the process. "So what would refract these lights so strangely and spectacularly?"

"Well, for one thing, a very large diamond," said Kailish, looking sober but excited.

"Large?" said Jessie. "These lights . . . that would take something that would make the Kohinoor diamond look like a grain of sand."

"Assuming it's a diamond," said Hadji. "It could be just a very large crystal array." His dark eyebrows shot up. "You know, I believe I have an appropriate analysis program on my laptop."

"Yeah," said Jonny. "And it's about time to see if we can jack into headquarters back home."

They took Kailish with them back up to their suite of rooms to continue the discussion. Jonny also told him about their run-in with Hyde-Pierce and Doodle, where the two were staying, and why they might mean trouble.

As soon as he unlocked the door, Jonny knew there was something wrong. The place looked as though it had been trashed by a rock group.

Hadji rushed to the desk. He slapped the polished wood with frustration and turned back to the group.

"Our laptops! They're *gone*."

5

"OUR *COMPUTERS?*" SAID JESSIE FRETFULLY. "YOU'RE SURE they're not here?"

"Absolutely," said Hadji. "They've been stolen."

"But we were just here an hour ago. . . ." Jonny thought quickly. "Hurry! The thief may still be in the building."

He almost ran over the stunned Kailish in his haste to get out to the hall. As he left the room he heard the whoosh and clank of an elevator door closing. Jonny sprinted as fast as he could. He arrived at the elevator just in time to catch a glimpse of a chunky hand and arm gripping three top-of-the-line notebook computers.

Then the door clamped shut.

"It's him. The thief!" cried Jonny.

He slammed his hand against the elevator buttons, hoping to stop the car's descent. He looked up at the lights above the shaft. No go. The elevator was still heading down.

And there wasn't another elevator car anywhere near their floor.

"Down the stairs!" he cried. "He's heading for the lobby."

Before anyone else could move, Jonny slammed through the door below the exit sign and hurried down the stairs.

They were on the eighth floor. Jonny was in good shape, and he took the flights of steps quickly. He could hear Jessie and Hadji pounding down right behind him.

At the lobby level he ran out of the stairwell.

The desk clerk looked up from some paperwork, a puzzled expression on his face.

"A man with an armful of computers," Jonny shouted to him. "Did he run through here?"

"No."

"There's been a robbery. Call the police, please. Is there another way out of the hotel on another floor?"

"Yes. The lower lobby."

Jonny turned and ran back down the stairs, almost running into Hadji. "He's probably heading for the exit on the lower level. We've got to catch him, Hadji."

"My personal journal is on my laptop!" said Jessie.

"Hot reading," said Jonny with a quick grin. "Must be why they swiped it." Without waiting for a reply, he almost jumped down the rest of the stairs.

Jonny scanned the lower lobby, which had a restaurant and meeting rooms. He noticed that the revolving door at the far end was swinging quickly, and he ran for it. He was happy he'd worn his tennis shoes that day. Of course, he almost *always* wore cool sneakers with the Quest Team design on them.

He whipped through the doors as fast as he dared and then pounded down to the busy street. At the edge of the road he stopped and looked both ways. He caught a glimpse of the man with the laptops escaping around the corner.

He couldn't make out anything other than that the man was big—and for a big man, he could move very fast. Jonny didn't waste any time analyzing the situation, but struck out after the guy.

"Jonny!" cried Jessie, coming through the revolving doors.

"Hurry! This way!" He loped after the man. Jonny was an athlete at school, and under ordinary circumstances he would have been able to catch up with the man in a very short time. However, because of the busy street—cars and pedestrians and even cattle roamed freely—he was forced to slow down.

A beggar crawled up and held out a hand.

"Watch it!" cried Jonny. Instead of going around him, he leaped *over* him.

The beggar hit the dirt, hands over his old head, and shouted after the crazy boy. He turned just in time to see two more teenagers coming at him.

"Yiiiiiiii!" the man shrieked as Hadji and Jessie bounded over him and continued to run after Jonny. The old beggar decided to call it a day. He tucked his alms into a dirty pocket and went back home.

Meanwhile, Jonny saw where the man with their computers was going.

The bazaar!

Good grief, Jonny thought. What with all the hustle and bustle there, the man would just be swallowed up. There would be no hope at all of catching him if he got too deep in there.

Jonny quickened his pace, careening around women in saris and dodging little barbecues where skewers of vegetables were roasting. He ran quickly down a clear stretch, leaping up now and then to see if he could catch sight of the man above the heads of all the people in the market.

There he was, lumbering heavily up the main way. Only instead of dodging people, the thief was plowing right through them, knocking some down as well.

Jonny recognized the khaki suit the guy wore. It *had* to be Higgins Doodle!

"Stop! Thief!" he cried at the top of his lungs.

The running man did not stop. However, many startled eyes looked up from the crowd. People scattered.

Jonny bashed into a fruit stall, scattering mangoes everywhere. "Sorry," he called over his shoulder. Curses followed him as he hurried forward.

Up ahead, a fakir in a turban was doing a firewalking display. He was walking barefooted over a large bed of hot coals.

The big man, with their laptops tucked under one arm, barreled straight through the coals.

"Cor! Ouch! Ouch! Blimey!" he cried. By the time he was through, his shoes were smoking.

Jonny turned sharply, changing his course to avoid the wide bed of coals. But suddenly a yapping dog appeared from nowhere, and Jonny tripped over it. Trying desperately to regain his balance, he staggered toward the edge of the coals.

Then he started to fall—and he could feel the searing heat of the hungry red fire reaching up for him.

6

JONNY QUEST FELL.

Someone screeched; someone else screamed.

He teetered over the coals, trying with all his might to twist and yank himself out of harm's way.

Gravity, though, pulled him down.

At the last moment hands grabbed him. They changed the angle of his plunge so that he landed on the edge of the coals. He got himself smudged and sooty—but not burned.

He looked up. Jessie hovered above him, mussed and concerned. "Jonny, are you all right?"

"The guy with our computers. Where is he?"

"He is lost to sight," said Hadji. "He is long gone, I fear."

"What a way to start a mission!" said Jonny. He got up and brushed himself off. "And Dad was going to let *us* be in charge of computing on this mission."

"He hasn't got his laptop with him?" said Jessie.

Jonny shook his head mournfully.

Hadji looked hopeful. "Maybe Kailish and the Indian

ministry have a laptop and modem that we might borrow."

"Yeah, but it won't have my journal on it," said Jessie. She shook her head. "I just hope whoever stole it gets some thrills out of it."

"I think I know who that someone is," said Jonny. "And he already gave us his address."

Dr. Benjamin Hyde-Pierce was just sitting down to a room service meal of sautéed monkey brains and chutney when Higgins Doodle burst through the hotel door.

"Good Lord," said Hyde-Pierce. "What have you got there?"

Doodle grinned a sly but goofy grin. "I bagged their computers, I did."

Hyde-Pierce's eyes gleamed. He took the silk napkin from his lap and stood. He beckoned for his henchman to place the stolen goods on the table before him. "Excellent. Good work." He opened the top of one and booted it up. "What else did you find out?"

"I eavesdropped on 'em awhile before I broke into their rooms, guv'nor," Doodle puffed. "Far as I can tell, they know nothing important."

"And that is how it should be—for now," said Hyde-Pierce. "Excellent. That will save us time we would otherwise have to spend exterminating them. However, if they should become pests again—" The computer beeped, interrupting them. Hyde-Pierce looked down.

On the color screen was a graphic that read: QUESTWORLD. ANNEX ONE. PLEASE ENTER PASSWORD.

The cursor blipped expectantly.

"Drat," said Hyde-Pierce. "Oh, well, it was to be expected. I dare say Frankenstein's Mother—our computer—will be able to crack the password, don't you think?"

"Oh, right, sir. Undoubtedly. I figured we might be able to find out something more about this fabled team."

"You did well, Higgins. You did very well indeed. Now why don't you take these down to the van and lock them up tight? I suspect that we may have visitors soon."

Doodle looked sheepish. "Unfortunately, guv'nor, that might be true. The little so-and-so spotted me and gave chase."

"I surmised as much from all your huffing, Higgins. No matter. Besides, I should like to have another talk with Master Quest—on my own territory. Hurry, though, and get these computers out of sight; we'll deal with them later. When you are finished, come back and observe. If the young people become too insistent, their ears may have to be boxed."

"Right," said Doodle, thumping his chest with a fist. "And I'm the man for that job. They're annoying little twerps."

"Gave you a good chase, did they, Doodle? Clever of you to shake them off, though. Well, be off with you."

The cockney hurried away to do as he was told. Hyde-Pierce sat back down and began to eat his meal.

"Monkey brains! Delicious! A true delicacy," he murmured.

But the food was not why he had come to this exotic country. There were far greater prizes to be had . . . and they would be his soon. Anyone who dared stand in his way would not live long enough to regret it!

At one time Hyde-Pierce had been content to follow the old, standard paths of scientific investigation. But it wasn't long before he had realized that little minds had constructed those paths, conforming to old, outdated values. If he stayed on those paths, he knew, he would also stay very, very poor, a slave to dilapidated university equipment. No, a mind like Hyde-Pierce's was meant for greater things . . . and far more riches!

There was a loud knock on the door.

Hyde-Pierce took his napkin and daintily dabbed at his mouth. "Now, whoever could *that* be?" he said softly. His chuckle sounded more like the growl of a predator.

The door opened.

"My goodness. What a surprise!" said Hyde-Pierce. "Change your mind, Jonny?"

"We need to talk to you," said Jonny.

"Why, of course, of course. Please, *do* come in." With the exaggerated gestures of an English gentleman, Hyde-Pierce beckoned them in.

Jonny looked at his companions. Both Jessie and

Hadji braced themselves and nodded. They were ready.

"All right, Doctor. But I should tell you that I've notified hotel security that we've come up here, and we're supposed to check in with them in fifteen minutes."

Hyde-Pierce blinked innocently. "You are fearful of dull old *moi?* How upsetting. Do come in and let me play host. I look forward to working with you, Jonny." He stepped away so they could enter.

"That's not exactly what we had in mind, Dr. Hyde-Pierce," said Jonny. "We—"

An overwhelming roar interrupted him.

He spun around.

There, in the middle of the hotel room, was a tiger, crouched and ready to spring.

7

Behind him, Jessie gasped, staring at the tiger.

It was a Bengal tiger, perhaps not as big as they often came but big enough to rip them apart. Its eyes glittered in the room light, and its mouth was open, showing huge, sharp fangs.

It didn't move any farther toward them.

It just sat down and regarded them.

"Good day, people," the tiger seemed to say.

"What—?" said Hadji.

Jonny spoke even as the realization struck him. "It's tame!"

"Oh, I'm so sorry. My little prank has frightened you," said Hyde-Pierce. "Ventriloquism is a little hobby of mine." He marched over to the big cat and stroked its fur. "Meet Mrs. Thatcher. On loan from a friend here. Very easy to manage—providing you've been properly introduced to the creature by its owner, as Higgins and I have. I thought it would be amusing to have a pet for my stay here. Say hello, Mrs. Thatcher."

A British woman's voice responded, though the tiger's jaw did not move. "Welcome to an important relic of the British Empire. There will always be an England—and not just in England!"

"That's right, you know," said Hyde-Pierce. "As long as we true British keepers of the faith move out upon the world—nay, upon the universe—our ideals will remain!"

"You mean the ideals of conquest and imperialism and pain?" said Hadji.

"I am a scientist. I do not deal with any of those. So, please have a seat. Shall I call room service? Tea? Biscuits? Monkey brains with chutney?" Hyde-Pierce smiled politely.

The tiger growled softly but did not approach them.

"We're not here to help you with whatever you're doing in India," said Jessie. "We're here to get our laptop computers back."

"I'm sorry. I don't understand," said Hyde-Pierce.

"Our hotel rooms. . . they've been ransacked," said Jonny. "Our computers are gone. And I chased a man who looked a lot like your Mr. Doodle."

"Higgins? Laptop computers? Why would he want your computers?"

"To cripple us . . . to get information," said Hadji. "Maybe just for the fun of it. I don't know."

Hyde-Pierce tsk-tsked. "I had so hoped that we would be able to cooperate. And now you make these upsetting charges. Mrs. Thatcher, what do you think?"

"We are not amused," said the tiger stiffly.

"There you go. My opinion exactly." He turned

36

back to Jonny. "Now, do you intend to be more civilized, or shall I have to demand that you go?"

"Oh, we'll go all right," said Jonny. "I didn't really expect you to 'fess up, Doctor. I just wanted to let you know that we're on to you."

"And maybe catch you red-handed," said Jessie.

"That's right," said Jonny. "I'm not naive enough to think you'll just fold your tent and leave—I only thought it was the fair thing to give you a chance to give us our computers back and get out."

"The Indian authorities have been notified," said Hadji.

"This is most alarming," said Hyde-Pierce. "You have no proof. No proof at all. And yet you come rushing in here with these ridiculous charges. We're scientific investigators, just like you, Jonny. You think you're the only ones who've heard of these mysterious lights in the Ranthambhore Preserve?"

"We're the only ones who have been authorized to investigate," said Jonny. "And you have to have permission to go into the area."

Hyde-Pierce shrugged. "We can observe the lights in other ways . . . and we have applied for permission."

"The only reason I can see why you'd want to work with us is so that you can ride our coattails into the preserve," said Hadji. "Believe me, our suspicions will be reported."

"Hmmm," said Hyde-Pierce. "What do you say to all this, Mrs. Thatcher?"

The tiger spoke, although now Jonny could see just

a trace of movement in Hyde-Pierce's prominent Adam's apple. "Perhaps it would be best for these children to be wary of where they go in that jungle. Perhaps they should have experienced help."

"I could not have said it better myself," said Hyde-Pierce. "I've done time not only in the jungles of India, you see, but also in those of Africa and New Guinea. I know my way about, and I strongly suspect that you will be in great danger in that preserve. Great danger indeed, without our help."

"You listen to 'im, kids," said a booming voice from behind them. "'E's right. These jokers from the government . . . rank amateurs in the jungle. Me, I know the jungle better than the East End of London!"

Jonny and the others wheeled around.

Standing in the doorway, blocking their exit, was Higgins Doodle, looking like a cat that just ate the canary and was now sizing up more appetizing prey.

"And I've shot my share of beasties like that one, I 'ave," continued the bulky cockney.

Mrs. Thatcher growled. "Yikes! I'm so scared."

Both Doodle and Hyde-Pierce laughed as though this were the greatest joke in the world.

Jonny was undeterred. "I bet you think there's a big diamond out there. I know the way your type thinks."

"Oh, do you now? You think that I'm looking for riches?" Hyde-Pierce sighed. "If only they would believe me, Higgins. Why, just this morning I was telling you what I hoped to achieve from this investigation."

"Knowledge. And vindication in the scientific

38

community," pronounced Doodle, holding himself up like a proper gentleman's gentleman. "That, and peace on earth."

"Peace on earth most of all," said Hyde-Pierce, cupping his hands in a prayerful attitude. His eyes turned up toward heaven.

"Oh, please. Peace on earth?" Jessie said scornfully.

"Doodle," said Jonny, "I saw you with those computers. You know I saw you. Now give them back. Right away."

Higgins shook his head. "I 'aven't got the least idea what you're talking about, lad. But I do have something I'd like to give you." He put his hand in his jacket pocket.

It came out holding a gun.

8

IT WAS A BLACK, GRIM-LOOKING GUN.

Its muzzle was pointed directly at Jonny's face.

"Good grief, Higgins," cried Dr. Hyde-Pierce. "What do you think you're doing?"

"I'm just—oof!"

The big man was hit hard from behind. He went down onto the floor like a sack of rice, and the gun clattered away. Within a moment the man who had tackled him had him in a hammerlock, and Doodle could not move.

The man was lean and muscular in jeans, black leather jacket, shades, and a crew cut.

"Dad!" said Jessie.

"Race!" said Hadji.

Jonny quickly picked up the gun that had fallen away from Doodle.

"'Ere! Wait a minute!" said the cockney henchman.

"Unhand that man!" said Hyde-Pierce imperiously. "Or I shall have to unleash the wrath of Mrs. Thatcher!"

The tiger growled.

Suddenly a small object barreled past Race and Doodle, yapping and barking madly. It stood valiantly between Jonny and the tiger, which had just risen to its feet again and looked about to attack.

It was Bandit, his hackles high, barking madly.

The tiger reared back. Uncertainly and perhaps even fear showed in its eyes.

"My, my, a tasty lunch for Mrs. Thatcher," said Hyde-Pierce. "But people, please! This is all so unnecessary. Violence! I shudder at the thought."

"It was only a practical joke," said Doodle in a quavering voice. "I surely didn't mean no 'arm. The gun, Master Quest. Look at that gun. It's not loaded!"

John checked the clip in the Beretta handgun. Sure enough, it was empty. "That's right." He looked down at their dog. "Bandit! Come here."

The dog growled unflinchingly at the tiger but then obeyed his master, stepping around and then behind Jonny, to where he was pointing. But the dog with the black mask over his eyes looked around and met the tiger's gaze stare for stare, as though daring the huge cat to make a move . . . just one little move!

"You see?" said Doodle. "Just 'aving meself a little bit of fun."

"Fun?" boomed a deep, commanding voice from beyond the room. "That's hardly a word I associate with you two criminals."

A tall man with a beard stepped into the room. He was wearing a khaki outfit and looked like the commander of some large army, with his steely gaze addressing all.

Dr. Benton Quest had just made his appearance.

"Why, what an honor, Dr. Quest," said Hyde-Pierce. "I had hoped that our next meeting would be less . . . dramatic. Still, perhaps we can negotiate. I tell you what: You have your flunky let my assistant up, and I won't allow Mrs. Thatcher to eat your pathetic little dog."

Bandit barked defiantly.

"If Bandit is hurt, you'll rue the day, Hyde-Pierce!" said Dr. Quest. "Nonetheless, there's no reason to have him down there like that, Race. Let him up."

"Sure, Doc. Whatever you say." Race let the big guy up.

Doodle lumbered to his feet, giving Race a wary look but seeming quite cheerful nonetheless. "Thanks, mate. Sorry about the misunderstanding. No 'ard feelings, eh? Looked like I had a gun on your friends . . . I understand that you were just trying to rescue them. That's what you been doing all your life, and that's what you were doin' now. I understand."

"Shut up," said Race. "Listen to what Dr. Quest has to say."

Dr. Quest took another two solid steps into the room. An aura of authority surrounded his handsome and dashing appearance. "So, Hyde-Pierce. We meet again. Not a happy day for me."

"Oh, dear me, Benton. Do dispense with all the drama and rigmarole. You must have guessed that two such bright and—er—inquisitive people would bump into each other again."

"I never thought of you as the inquisitive type,

Hyde-Pierce. More the *acquisitive* sort." One of Dr. Quest's eyebrows lifted mockingly. "I hope you got full value from what you stole from me."

"You cannot prove a thing, Dr. Quest," said Hyde-Pierce.

"That's right, not a bloody thing!" echoed Doodle.

"Well, that's not the issue now, though, is it?" said Dr. Quest. "The issue is what brings you to India."

"I think you know that very well, Dr. Quest," said Hyde-Pierce. "As I told your son, it is for the same reason you are here. In fact, I also made a suggestion to him—and I will make the same suggestion to you." He put his finger up into the air and smiled. "I strongly suggest that we work together on this matter of the strange lights near the so-called Forbidden City of Luxor."

"We'd have to be watching our backs all the time," said Race.

"Yes. Not a pleasant alliance." In his hand Dr. Quest held a cane. He lifted it now and pointed it at the other man of science. "I cannot stop you from making inquiries, but be advised: I will warn the Indian government of your past. And so beware, Dr. Hyde-Pierce, for they most certainly will be watching you."

"Advice taken. Just remember," said Hyde-Pierce, "you're the grumps. We're quite open to exchanging information at any time. Aren't we, Mrs. Thatcher?"

"Only if I get to eat the little dog!" said the tiger.

"Oh, and one more thing, Jonny Quest," Doodle said. He took an orange water pistol from his pocket and squirted the teenager. Then he turned to Race. "Be good to me, Race Bannon, or you'll be next."

Jonny wiped his face. "I can't imagine what else you got through customs, Doodle." He turned to the others. "I guess we've given our message . . . and gotten one as well."

"Calm down, mate! It was just a larf!" said Doodle, twirling the gun around his finger.

Hyde-Pierce made a "naughty, naughty" sign with his finger. "You must excuse my friend. He does enjoy those practical jokes. Now, Dr. Quest and team, since you won't join me, you might as well be going. I wish you the best of luck. May the best team crack this mystery first." He sighed melodramatically. "I only wish we could work together. Toodle-loo!"

"Come on, guys," said Jonny. "Let's get out of here."

"Farewell, brave junior scientists," said Mrs. Thatcher.

Jonny ignored the ventriloquism and stalked out. They were due to leave for the preserve the next day, and he wanted to straighten up the mess in their rooms and get some rest.

"I swear!" said the young boy. "I saw a god. I saw Kali, and she chased me from the Ranthambhore Preserve. Do not go there. It is a cursed place!"

It was evening. Dr. Quest and Race were out again, making preparations, and Jonny, Hadji, and Jessie had been about to call it a night when Kailish had brought them a visitor.

He was a boy named Ranjit.

Ranjit, with wide eyes full of wonder, told his story of how he'd gone out to look at the fantastic lights that had been springing up from the midst of the Ranthambhore Preserve. But he had been halted by a frightening creature.

"Kali!" said Hadji. "The goddess of death."

"Ah, yes, we know," put in Jessie. "We've seen *Gunga Din*."

"I hope you do not judge our country by nineteen-thirties movies made in Hollywood," said Kailish.

"No, of course not," said Jonny. "Jessie is just being smart-alecky. I believe she's displaying what is called in our country 'rationalist's doubt.'"

"There's no evidence of the existence of gods or ghosts," said Jessie. "I have a scientific attitude."

The young boy pointed at his eyes. "With these I saw it, *memsahib*. These eyes have never lied to me before. Please, do not go into that evil place. The gods are at work there and have given me a vision—I must warn all to stay away. Stay away from the lights."

Hadji said, "Thank you, my friend. We truly appreciate your concern. However, there have been other sightings of strange things in the forests of Ranthambhore, is this not true?"

"Yes, indeed. But I did not believe them then. I most certainly do now," said the boy. He nervously slurped the Coke they had given him.

"However, no one has been hurt by these visions," countered Hadji.

"No. Not yet. But no one has yet dared to go very far toward the lights after they have seen these things, either," said the boy.

"What do you think, Jonny?" said Kailish. "Do you think this is all part of the phenomenon?"

"You have no pictures of these apparitions?"

"No. But as you saw, we *do* have pictures of the Luxor lights—and they seem to be connected with these apparitions."

"Yes. Either they are an aftereffect—or something perhaps even stranger and more diabolical," said Jonny.

"What do you mean?"

"I'll explain it to you later, Kailish," said Jonny. He shook the young boy's hand. "Thank you so much for taking the time to come and tell us these things. I promise we will do our very best to solve this puzzle."

Both Jessie and Hadji graciously thanked the boy as well.

But Ranjit looked upset as he walked out, still clinging to his can of soda pop. "I warn you, my friends," he said, eyes wide. "I was an unbeliever once and now am no longer. There are worse things than dying, and those things may happen to you if you venture into the preserve!"

9

"DR. QUEST! WATCH OUT!"

Race Bannon pushed Jonny's father out of the way and ducked himself, just in the nick of time.

A large knife slammed into the wall behind them, point first.

The evil-looking thing vibrated with its impact. Jonny could see that if it had hit his father, it would have gone straight through him and come out the other side.

Bandit barked, blunt nose pointed up.

Jonny swung his head in that direction. For an instant he saw eyes—grim, evil eyes—staring down from the top of a low building. Eyes surrounded by black cloth.

"A ninja?" said Jessie.

"A pretty scruffy-looking ninja!" said Hadji. "No, a member of some sort of Indian secret society."

Dr. Quest brushed himself off. "We mustn't stand about and conjecture." He pointed his cane up. "Let's go after him—he's probably been hired by Hyde-

Pierce. If we can prove it, we can get the villain out of our hair."

Jonny and Race were already starting to run.

"Be careful!" cried Hadji. "They are dangerous!"

"No kidding," said Jessie, taking a look at the embedded knife.

Yapping, Bandit was soon at Jonny's heels.

It was the morning after the confrontation at the hotel, and preparations were being made for the trip into the Ranthambhore Preserve. They were supposed to leave that afternoon. Dr. Quest, however, had decided that everyone should take some time off for a relaxing lunch at a restaurant that he and Race had found the other day. So they had left their hotel for the short walk—and stumbled straight into this ambush!

"Up here!" cried Jonny. "A stairway!" Without waiting, Jonny charged up it. He was that kind of guy—a little reckless. Jonny's philosophy, however, was that sometimes you just had to take chances or you wouldn't get results.

His special Quest Team sneakers slapping on the old stone, Jonny raced up the steps. Bandit was just a little ahead of him. The dog was practiced in staying out of Jonny's way, and he was a welcome helper in this hunt.

"Be careful, Jonny!" cried Dr. Quest.

Race yelled, "We're right behind you, guy!"

The steps were sandy, and it was hard for Jonny to keep his balance, but he managed to scramble up them. Just as he huffed his way to the top, he caught sight of a man in loose clothing and a turban jumping across the gap to the next roof. It was only a four-foot jump, but it still looked dangerous.

"Stay, Bandit!"

The dog reluctantly obeyed, stopping at the edge but barking madly.

Without breaking stride, Jonny jumped.

He sailed easily over the edge and caught a whiff of garbage from the alley below.

He landed on the gravel of the next roof and skidded, but managed not to fall. He looked around. On the other side of the building was the man. He swung around. Seeing Jonny not far enough behind him for his liking, he reached into his black robes.

Jonny expected another knife, but he still kept on running, steeling his reflexes.

Instead a modern gun emerged.

Uh-oh, thought Jonny.

With lightning speed, the man raised the gun, aimed, and fired.

Jonny, though, had already changed course. He flung himself behind a primitive chimney. The bullet zipped through the air where he had been and slammed into the edge of the roof, kicking up a spray of rock.

Jonny kept on rolling, then suddenly changed his direction, rolling back the way he had come and picking up a palm-sized stone he'd noticed.

Without exposing much of himself, he stood up slightly and heaved the stone with every bit of the skill of a baseball pitcher.

The missile slammed directly into the man's hand,

and he shrieked. The gun went flying away over the side of the building. For just the slimmest of moments, the man seemed confused and stunned.

Jonny took the opportunity to hurl himself at the assassin. He slammed into the dark man, tackling him. But the momentary disorientation had worn off quickly, and even though Jonny was an excellent martial artist, trained by Race Bannon himself back at their headquarters in Maine, the dark man countered his move. He grabbed Jonny's arm and flung him toward the edge.

Jonny was hurled over.

Peripherally, he saw the dark man turn and actually *jump* down off the building himself. The man, however, most certainly had his jump under control. Jonny well knew that his own fall was uncontrolled and that it would be hard not to land on his head or elbow or something else breakable.

As he went over the edge Jonny desperately swung his body around and reached out with his hands for the edge of the roof.

One hand scrabbled off helplessly, and Jonny's stomach lurched.

However, the other hand hooked around the edge, and Jonny hung on for all he was worth. As his body slammed against the side of the wall, Jonny could see the dark form of the assailant scuttling off down the alley toward freedom.

Now that Jonny had righted himself, his first impulse was simply to leap off, land on his feet, and chase the guy.

However, something told him to look down.

Below him were shards of glass in a garbage dump, jagged edges sticking up. Scattered among the glass were planks of wood with long, rusty nails, the points facing up as well.

Not a good place to fall, no sirree.

With all his might, Jonny swung up to grab the edge of the roof with his free hand. However, the force of his effort caused some of the loose bricks to fall off, clattering down past his eyes.

He wouldn't be able to hang on for long.

Just then a small head peered over the edge.

"Bandit!"

The bulldog barked.

"Bandit, I need help. Get Race or Dad or—"

The dog didn't linger to listen to the rest of the sentence.

Jonny's grip slipped a little more. He was hanging on by his fingers now—and they hurt horribly. Yet he knew if he did anything more than just hang there, he'd slip off for sure.

Carefully he looked down. Maybe if he could land so that he didn't fall over, he could avoid—

A hand clamped his wrist.

"Hang in there, Jonny boy." Race's strong voice was the best thing he'd heard all day.

Race reached down with his other hand, found Jonny's forearm, and pulled him up and over the edge. Jonny scrabbled over.

The others were running toward them.

"Jonny! Are you okay?" asked Jessie.

"We heard a gunshot!" said Hadji.

"That was because this cult assassin had a handgun!" said Jonny.

"I wonder why he didn't use it on me," said Dr. Quest.

"The assassin cults prefer their murders to be as silent as possible," said Hadji.

"Unless they get desperate," added Race.

Jessie peered over the side. "Which way did he go?"

"Oh, he's long gone," said Jonny. "Who do you think . . ." He didn't finish his sentence.

Dr. Quest was frowning. "I *know* who hired that guy. It must have been Hyde-Pierce. Dr. Hyde-Pierce, it seems, would very much like us out of the picture here, which makes me wonder exactly how much— and just plain *how*—he's involved in this mystery!"

"That's just a complication, Dr. Quest," said Race, looking with admiration at his friend. "I'm sure you'll get to the bottom of it."

"Well, right now I think we'll get to the bottom of a relaxing lunch and then take a cab back to the hotel. We have an important meeting with Kailish, who is finalizing some last-minute matters. And then we're off to Ranthambhore."

"And the Forbidden City of Luxor," said Jonny.

Jessie shook her head. "Jonny, you just can't get enough of danger, can you?"

"Actually," said Jonny, "I really hate it—but it really likes me."

* * *

"Well, here we are," said Kailish. "All packed and ready to go."

Jonny and the Quest Team stood in the parking lot outside the hotel.

Smiling at them, and looking very proud of himself, was their guide from the Indian government, Kailish, alongside two Land Rovers, one red and the other black. They were sturdy four-wheel-drive vehicles, able to navigate the kind of terrain into which they were about to enter.

"You're sure you have everything we asked for?" said Dr. Quest.

"Yes, indeed, Dr. Quest." The Indian official handed over a checklist with a large number of items, all marked off. "In this Land Rover are the items you brought with you from the United States. In the other are the items the Indian government is supplying. It was great trouble to get them, but I am proud to say that I worked very hard."

Dr. Quest nodded. "Good. Well done."

"We've got a regular miniature caravan here," said Race, walking alongside the Land Rovers.

"Actually," said Dr. Quest, "I want to split the team for a few hours—for a very good reason." He turned to the others. "Race and I have already been to the Ranthambhore Preserve. We have a map, and we generally know our way around. So Race and I will take one of the Land Rovers and head straight to the spot where the boy Ranjit saw the Indian goddess Kali. We'll set up camp there. Kailish knows the area well also. I've asked him—and he's agreed—to drive you in the other Land Rover to see some of the highlights of the park." Dr. Quest smiled easily, loosening up a bit. "We don't just want you to see the sights, though. We want you to survey the area as you go and take notes if you see anything that's unusual or suspicious. The place where Ranjit saw the vision—the place where we'll all meet—is also a good spot from which to observe any appearance of the lights we're looking for." He cocked his head. "Does that sound all right to you?"

"Sure, Dad. But what about Bandit?" said Jonny.

Bandit barked and wagged his stumpy tail upon hearing his name.

"We'd like to take Bandit along with us," said Race. "He'll be an excellent early-warning system in the camp, when we set it up."

Bandit yipped, obviously delighted with the praise.

"Okay, but we'll miss him." Jessie leaned over and rubbed behind the dog's ears, just where he liked it.

"Right, then," said Dr. Quest. "Any questions?"

"Yes, Dr. Quest," said Hadji. "Just what exactly do you think is happening out there?"

"I'll have more of an idea, Hadji, after I make some observations and measurements at the campsite this evening." He frowned thoughtfully. "Whatever the answer is, though, I have the feeling it's something quite remarkable—and quite possibly something out of this world!"

Jonny shivered in anticipation.

Just his kind of adventure!

10

"THERE IT IS," SAID THEIR GUIDE, KAILISH. "RANTHAMBHORE Preserve."

Kailish had stopped their Land Rover on a rise that gave them a good view of the preserve.

"Wow," said Jessie. "It's beautiful."

"And it's huge as well," said Jonny. "The preserve stretches as far as the eye can see, right, Hadji?"

The ever-studious Hadji rustled his map, then squinted up into the sun. "As far as I can tell, it stretches a good deal farther."

Jonny got out and took a breath of fresh air. It smelled *alive*—alive with the smell of the rivers and lakes, the mountains, the plants and flowers.

But most of all, it smelled of the musky scent of wildlife. Birds, monkeys, cats . . . even the fish in the lakes probably contributed some kind of scent. It gave the panorama a particular and unique tang of excitement and adventure.

Each creature was comfortable in its particular biome—that is, a particular type of landscape. Deer roamed the plains in herds. Swamps were everywhere.

There was the jungle, of course, large swaths of the most intense green that Jonny had ever seen. It was just after the monsoon season, and the clouds had dumped large amounts of rain. That along with the rich rays of the sun had cooked up an amazing stew of vegetation.

In the distance were small mountains—or large hills, depending on one's point of view. Amid the hills were lakes, gleaming silver in the afternoon sun. The largest lake was the source of the strange lights. Just behind the lakes was the village of Ranjit, the boy who had told the story of seeing a strange apparition.

Jonny looked out over the preserve. Somewhere out there was the secret to the mystery of the spectacular light show Ranthambhore was giving off.

"I see what you mean, Kailish, about there being limited access to that lake," said Jessie, pulling out a set of binoculars and peering through them. "As far as I can tell, there's just one road . . . and that's iffy at best."

"Yes, at this time of year, after the monsoon, there is more plant life than can be easily handled. It chokes off everything," said the little man, taking out a red checked bandanna and dabbing at his brown forehead. It was not only hot out here, away from the air-conditioning of the Land Rover, but humid, too.

Jonny could take it. At least they were in the great wide open spaces. What he really hated were cities like Washington, D.C., and New York City, where you not only felt like you were in a pressure cooker but also were dumped in with a lot of other grumpy people.

"Believe me," said Kailish, sighing, "I would far rather take a small plane in there and land closer to the area where we believe the manifestations are taking place." He waved his bandanna with frustration. "But there is simply no strip long enough to land on." He shrugged. "No matter. I know the area very well. I have taken many visitors here, you see." He grinned amiably. "So you see, you not only get a mystery, my friends; you get a first-rate tour guide and driver."

He patted the pockets of his khaki jacket. "Oh, my. Oh, dear. Now where did I put my spectacles? I am not a legal driver without my spectacles."

"Um, Kailish . . . steady there," said Jonny. "They're on top of your head."

Their guide reached up carefully and tapped his dark curly hair. "Ah, yes. Of course," he said sheepishly. "There is so much to keep track of. So much!"

"Don't worry. Like I said, if anything goes wrong, *any* of us can drive," said Jonny.

"That is true," said Hadji. "Without licenses, however."

"Right," said Jessie with a grin. "Like the tiger cops are gonna pull us over and give us a ticket!"

"If there is any problem with wildlife–tigers, say" said Kailish, "we can always take refuge in the sturdy Land Rover!"

No, they'd be just fine, Jonny thought. They had absolutely everything they could possibly need. And

Jonny's dad and Race had the rest of the scientific equipment.

He wondered about his dad, There was another team vying for the knowledge they sought. A very *nasty* team.

How would Dr. Quest deal with them? He needed to understand that, to be able to make his own decisions.

Jonny glanced around, but there was no sign of fresh tire tracks, which would have meant that someone had arrived before they did. And on the drive in, he'd flashed a glance back from time to time to see if anyone was following them. He'd seen no one except for some long-beaked birds in a marshy area.

"We should be moving on," stated Kailish. "There are things I wish to show you—including the spot where Ranjit and the other villagers saw the strange apparitions. The place where we will meet your father."

"Yes, indeed," said Hadji. "It is my special desire to view this place."

"You bet," said Jessie. "Maybe there will be clues that will tie the lights in with this other phenomenon."

"I sure wouldn't doubt it," said Jonny. "So let's get going. Thanks for the stop-and-look, Kailish. It's startlingly beautiful."

"Ah!" said the man, eyes wide with enthusiasm. "Wait till you see what awaits us farther on!"

They piled back into the Land Rover, and Kailish started the engine again.

The man drove much more slowly than Jonny

would have, but he knew the area, Jonny reasoned. They passed a stand of trees, some plains, and a little clot of jungle. Then Kailish slowed down even more.

"Oh, dear," he said, peering over the steering wheel.

"What's wrong?" Jessie asked.

"This swampy area. It extends even farther than I had anticipated. Well, no matter. There is a firmer area just over here, I am very positive. And after all, this *is* an all-terrain vehicle."

He shifted gear and moved slowly and carefully— and suddenly stopped.

"Uh-oh," Kailish said.

"We're not stuck, are we?" said Jessie. There was a trace of annoyance and perhaps even fear in her voice.

Jonny couldn't blame her. This area looked kind of grim and nasty, with bent trees and reeds twisting all about. A foul stench was drifting in through the air intakes of the car.

"A tiny delay!" Kailish assured them. "No more."

He shifted down to first gear and started to rock the vehicle backward and forward.

"Ah, I see," said Kailish. "I detect the difficulty to be in the right rear wheel." He peered through the tinted windshield at the surrounding vegetation. "A very small matter, I quite assure you. All that is necessary is—" He pointed off to the right. "That branch over there. That should give our excellent treads the purchase they need to attain the next stage of our journey."

"You mean you want Hadji and me to go out there,

pick up the branch, and stick it under the wheel?" said Jonny.

"Don't you understand English?" said Jessie. "Look, I'll go with you and help. I'm in this as deep as you—and besides, it will also get rid of some of the weight in the car."

They got out.

Jonny's feet squelched as they sank into the mud, but fortunately they did not sink too far. "It's all right to stand on. But I gotta say, I wish I had some boots."

The others came out as well, and together they lifted the branch. They were just swinging it around toward the rear wheel when Jessie pointed off into the distance and gasped.

"Over there, guys!"

Jonny turned around. At first he couldn't see what she was talking about.

Then he saw the three crocodiles waddling their way.

11

WOOF!

Bandit was in Dr. Quest's lap, gazing out toward the fields and plains and trees of the Ranthambhore Preserve. A group of birds and monkeys sat in a huge vine-covered tree. Bandit wasn't barking; he knew better than that. He was just expressing his excitement at being out in the wild among all these fabulous animals.

"That's right, boy," said Dr. Quest, petting the dog as he peered through the windshield of the Land Rover. "But you'd better get used to all the birds and animals and keep a low profile." He sucked thoughtfully at his ever-present empty pipe.

"That's right, Bandit," said Race, his sturdy hands gripping the wheel of the vehicle professionally. "You're about the size of a small snack for some of these beasts."

Bandit whined and ducked his head a moment, as though thinking it over. Then he lunged forward toward the window.

Woof!

Birds flapped off from the tree. Monkeys skittered away.

Bandit turned around and looked at the ex–Navy SEAL with a hint of defiance, as though to say, *Oh, yeah? Well, I'm not afraid!*

Dr. Quest laughed. "Good for you, Bandit. But you probably want to be careful anyway."

The dog leaned his head out the window again, dreamily looking out at the beautiful land.

"Dr. Quest," began Race thoughtfully. He squared his huge shoulders and kept a careful eye on the narrow dirt track that had to suffice as a road here. "Do you think it was wise to let the others go on that tour on their own?" His face looked grim, perhaps even a little worried.

"We have to remember that all of them—Jonny, Hadji, and Jessie—aren't kids anymore," Dr. Quest replied. "They're young adults. If you make them feel as though you've got to be their escort all the time, they'll rebel. They won't feel trusted, and they won't have the independence they crave."

"Yeah, but I'm afraid they're going to get into trouble."

"You're being a good father and a good friend," said Dr. Quest. "But you have to let go. One of my nine advanced degrees, remember, is in psychology, but I really don't need it to know that kids their age need to feel independent sometimes."

"Yes, I guess you're right," said Race. "I do admire you, Dr. Quest. You're not only smart, you're wise."

Dr. Quest's smile split his beard. "Besides, this way,

when we make camp, we can get some good, concentrated work done."

The breeze from the preserve was full of rich smells. "It's good to be back here again," said Race. "They say this place is doing what it was intended to do. Not just the tiger population is returning, but many other species of wildlife are increasing in number as well."

"Yes, Race. It's good to see a place without the ugly mark of mankind on it. To think of all those years when hunters shot everything in sight—not for food or in self-defense, but just to kill things. I worry so much about the human race. We kill and we pollute . . . I think everyone should see what nature is like without mankind's mark. I guess that's why I wanted Kailish to take the rest of the team on that tour."

Race smiled—an unusual event. It was like a storm cloud lifting. "Good thing he did. I doubt you could have resisted lecturing the kids that way."

Dr. Quest laughed. "Yes, that's true. Let Kailish lecture them this time."

"What do you think is really out there, Doc?" asked Race, frowning again and looking out past the hills that concealed the lake from which the lights emanated.

"I've been making some calculations, Race, from readings already gathered. I'm not yet prepared to state anything positively, but I do have theories. I—"

Suddenly there was a whapping sound from above them. At first the sound was small, but it grew louder . . . then *very* loud.

Bandit woofed and looked up.

63

"Sounds like a chopper," said Race. "You want to get a visual on that, Doc?"

"Right," said the scientist. "Bandit, backseat!"

The dog obeyed, scurrying out of the way. Once in the backseat, he jumped up and peered out one of the side windows.

Dr. Quest took off his seat belt and looked up into the sky. Despite the sunglasses he wore, the glare of the sun was blinding. But then a large form covered the sun—a form topped with whirring blades.

Whop-whop-whop!

"It's a helicopter, all right."

"Indian government, do you think?" shouted Race above the noise. "Are they trying to attract our attention?"

"That would be the logical explanation. Maybe we'd better pull off and see."

Race stopped the Land Rover, and Dr. Quest leaned out and waved at the dark shadow. He saw a brief glint of metal, then heard a bang. A bullet whistled past his head and whacked into the road.

Someone was shooting at them!

Quickly he pulled his head back into the Land Rover. "Rifle fire."

"I don't see any cover, Doc."

"Up ahead—that copse of trees. If we can pull in there," cried Dr. Quest, "I think we'll have a chance."

"It's Hyde-Pierce, isn't it, Dr. Quest?"

"Or a hireling," said the bearded scientist grimly. "I just wish I knew why he was so intent on stopping us."

Another bullet ricocheted off the top of the Land Rover.

"The radio," Race suggested.

"Yes, of course," said Dr. Quest, grabbing for the radio. He pulled the receiver away from the set and clicked it on. It was already set for the frequency of the radio in Kailish's Land Rover.

But all the two men heard was static.

Dr. Quest fiddled with it. A squealing erupted. He recognized the sound.

Race did, too. "We're being jammed!" the former Navy tech expert exclaimed. "We can't communicate!"

"Those trees—we'll have a chance in those trees," said Dr. Quest.

Three more bullets thwacked into the top of the Rover. One penetrated, smacking into the backseat right by Bandit. The dog tilted his head up and growled defiantly.

Race stepped on the gas, weaving as much as he could to avoid the bullets. "Hang on!" he cried above the roar of the engine. "And hang on to Bandit, too. Evasive action approaching!"

"Bandit—up here, boy!" called Dr. Quest.

The dog leaped immediately into Dr. Quest's arms, and Jonny's father clasped the animal tightly.

Race slammed on the brakes, and the Land Rover screeched to a near halt. The helicopter chasing them, though, did not have brakes. It continued on overhead.

"Okay, down that trail!" said Dr. Quest, pointing.

"Right, Doc." Race jammed his foot on the accelerator again, spun the wheel, and peeled out. A rooster tail of dust grew behind them as they hurtled down the track in their new direction.

"The grove of trees isn't far," said Dr. Quest. "But watch out for the ditch along this side."

"Gotcha, Doc," said Race, concentrating intently on his driving.

Meanwhile the helicopter banked, carving out a wide circle that brought it back around in their direction. It started descending toward them.

"It's comin' straight at us, Doc."

"Race, just get to those trees and we'll figure out what to do from there," said Dr. Quest. The shoulder harness and lap belt had kept him firmly placed in his seat when they'd stopped a few moments before, and they would have to do so again. "Just take any necessary evasive action!"

The sleek black helicopter continued its pursuit, hurling itself at them like some demon of the air. Rifle fire spat from its side. A bullet crashed into the Land Rover's windshield, causing a spiderweb of cracks to radiate from the impact point. Race flinched slightly but kept the wheel steady.

Up ahead, tantalizingly close, the cover of trees beckoned.

Crack! Crack!

More bullets.

Several struck the front of the vehicle, puncturing both front tires. The Land Rover slewed off the trail wildly.

"Race!" cried Dr. Quest. "The ditch! Watch out for the—"

Race yanked on the wheel with all his might, but the Land Rover continued its skid. For a seemingly endless moment it hung over the edge of the ditch—and then tumbled down the steep ten-foot incline, smashing to a catastrophic rest at the bottom.

12

LOOK AT THAT MOUTH, THOUGHT JONNY. *IT COULD CRUSH A teenager in one bite.*

As though to illustrate, the crocodile snapped its mouth closed with a fleshy *whap*. Water splashed over the other crocodiles.

"Kailish!" cried Hadji.

Kailish turned around to see what was going on and did a double take. Then he leaned out the window. "Do not worry. Their teeth are not very sharp."

The reptiles, fortunately, had slowed down. Perhaps they had been attracted by the three youngsters and then upon seeing the Land Rover thought it was some older, much more frightening brother.

An interesting thought.

"Oh, that's okay, then," said Jessie sarcastically. "Me, I think I'm going to get back into the car, if you don't mind."

"Perhaps we should just speak softly," said Hadji. "And wave our big stick."

One of the crocodiles hissed at them, showing a terrifying reptilian gullet. It was the largest of the three, maybe nine feet long and thick around the middle. Probably well fed, too, Jonny figured, what with all the pickings in the river and the surrounding swamps. Still, the hissing crocodile seemed to like the scent of human flesh. It, like its fellows, had hard, knobby gray-brown flesh and evil, ancient eyes.

Somehow it didn't look real . . . yet it most certainly was. And unfortunately all the crocodiles smelled of their last fishy dinner.

"Ah, that's right, you've been reading American history, haven't you, Hadji?" said Jonny. "Well, it's worth a try. We can't just stay inside the Rover while the crocodiles circle. All together now—heave!"

As a team, they managed to throw the large branch. Parts of it hit the crocodiles in various parts of their anatomies.

The large beasts backed away, as though to reassess their situation. Their eyes betrayed no feeling whatsoever. It seemed as if they operated by some strange combination of instinct and need.

"Good. Good job," called Kailish. "Now place your hands to your ears!"

None of them questioned the order.

No sooner had Jonny clapped his hands over his ears than Kailish slammed on the Land Rover's horn. It was like no other horn that Jonny had ever heard before; the noise made his teeth vibrate. Birds burst out from nearby trees and flapped away.

The eyes of the crocodiles widened ever so slightly, but the creatures did not move.

"Oh, blast it!" said Kailish. He pulled out a high-powered rifle, aimed, and shot the most aggressive crocodile dead.

The other crocodiles started backing away, and then, in their slinking reptilian fashion, they turned and swished away, their huge tails causing waves in the shallow water.

Every bit of wildlife in the area must have been scared off by the horn and the gun, which was fine with Jonny.

"Good job, Kailish," said Jonny. "Too bad you had to kill one. But of all the animals out here, why is it that the first kind we run across is the kind I hate the most?"

"The best manner in which to run across a crocodile," stated Hadji in a monotone, "is while inside a very large tank."

Kailish shook his head sorrowfully. "Crocodiles kill you by grabbing you in their massive jaws and dragging you deep into the water. The water here is very shallow. Still, it looked as though they were going to try. I hate to destroy any living thing, but I had to protect you."

"Thanks. We realize that," said Jessie. "And that's a great anti-croc siren you've got there. Too bad it didn't work."

"It was worth a try," said Kailish. "Now, perhaps you might attempt the business with the stick again. I believe that it holds much promise to extricate us from here."

This time it worked. Within a few minutes the Land Rover was out of its muddy trap and back on drier ground, rolling along.

70

"Ah, excellent," pronounced Kailish, grinning happily. "You see, the preserve may have its predators, but if handled properly, there is no problem whatsoever."

Jonny looked down at himself and then at his companions. There were all half soaked and spattered with mud.

"Pay no heed, my friends," said Kailish. "It is merely good Indian soil. It will dry and flake off soon enough. If not, we will be by a lake shortly and you may wash yourselves. We do have towels." He smiled kindly. "We have everything we could need."

The Rover drove through a break in the foliage. Here the vague indentation in the forest looked faintly more like a road. They continued for a while in silence.

"Now you will see something very important, very stunning," Kailish told them as the group topped the crest of a hill.

As she caught sight of what lay below them, Jessie exclaimed, "Oh, my goodness!"

"Ditto," said Jonny, awed.

13

STANDING BEFORE THEM WERE SOME OF THE MOST UNIQUE RUINS that Jonny had ever seen.

"The Fortress of Ranthambhore itself," said Kailish. "Over a thousand years old. Quite a sight, is it not?" He nodded to Hadji. "Perhaps our ancestors fought together side by side in this fortress, Hadji."

"Or perhaps they fought one another," said Hadji.

Kailish grinned. "One can only hope."

The crumbling buildings were scattered over the hills. Trees and bushes sprouted in and around the ruins, and vines and creepers curled through their jagged walls and facades. Half-gone towers rose up from the ground. Parapets loomed here and there, lofting majestically over all.

"Ancient India truly had a unique architecture," commented Jessie.

"Yes, and this is just the edge. The fortress is several miles in circumference. It is known that even the great Mogul emperor Akbar laid siege to these walls." The guide sighed. "Now look who rules."

He pointed to a family of monkeys playing along a wall.

"Langurs. The only type of primate in the preserve, curiously enough," said Kailish.

"Except for us," said Jonny.

Jessie arched an eyebrow. "Some of us are more monkeyish than others."

"Perhaps if we are lucky," said Kailish, "we will be able to see a leopard . . . or even a tiger. They are free to roam the ruins, of course. The archaeologists have long since come and gone."

"Is this like the Forbidden City of Luxor?" asked Jessie.

"In some ways, yes, but in others . . ." Kailish stopped. "Well, you will see that place later. It is by the lake. Then you can decide for yourselves."

They took a moment to sip some of the *chai* they'd brought along. However, neither leopards nor tigers made an appearance while they were there.

"Don't worry, my friends. Be not disappointed. I promise you, we will see some soon. A tiger, at the very least."

Jonny wasn't sure if he really wanted the prediction to come true.

They moved on toward the setting sun.

Along the way, Kailish pointed out some of what Ranthambhore was actually preserving.

"There are more than three hundred kinds of trees in the area," said their guide. "Fifty aquatic plants, a hundred species of herbs, two hundred and seventy-two species of birds, twelve species of reptiles and amphibians, twenty-two species of mammals . . . and, my goodness, I don't quite remember how many kinds of grasses and vines and such there are."

"I want my money back!" said Jonny. They laughed and continued onward.

Kailish drew their attention to some of the many varieties of flora and fauna along the side of the road and in a small shallow lake they passed. There were not only the kinds of deer that they'd seen grazing before, sambars and chitals, but also cinkaqs, which were Indian gazelles, and nilgais, a species of antelope that their guide told them was also called a blue bull.

"Ah, Master Tiger adores these for his dinner. But they are swift, all of them, and good with their horns or antlers. The tiger must use much power and precision in his attack or it will be for naught. And many times the tiger will fail . . . many more times than he will succeed." Kailish nodded vigorously. "This, I think, is a great lesson in perseverance for all of us. For without the greatest of perseverance, there would be no tigers."

"They were almost wiped out, right?" said Jonny. "That's why this preserve is here."

"Gee," said Jessie, "you must have read the same book I did."

Jonny gave Jessie a dirty look. He'd only been trying to give Kailish the opportunity to give his lecture. Why did Jessie give him such a hard time? She was always on his case lately!

Kailish did not seem to take offense. "Yes. Tigers have been hunted for centuries by the maharajas of India. However, the hunt was far more equal when it was with spear and arrow. When the English came, they brought with them the rifle. That, and constant hunting, brought the tiger population very low. And tiger bones are valuable, to say nothing of tiger skins. Fortunately, our people realized that something had to be done. Hence such preserves as this were established. At the time Ranthambhore was opened, the tiger stayed away from man. He hunted only at night. After a few years, however, the tiger population grew, and the tiger again hunted by day—and could also be observed by day. It was wonderful news indeed for our nation." Kailish looked about. "Alas, Master Tiger is not showing himself much for you, our honored guests. Sometimes you can just see them strolling along in the fields. They hardly take notice anymore of our vehicles."

Kailish continued to point out other wildlife. He showed them beautifully plumed peacocks, babblers, parakeets, and myna birds. He named some of the trees—pipals, mangoes, jamuns—but the tree that fascinated Jonny the most was the banyan tree.

These vast, gnarled trees looked like many trees combined in a twisted, sprawling mess. The banyans were topped with masses of green leaves, and they grew over boulders or rocks or ruins—they simply spread anywhere they possibly could.

"This tree," said Kailish, "is one of the oldest. It is hundreds and hundreds of years old."

"Kind of like our redwood trees in California," said Jonny.

"In age, perhaps, but the banyan tree has a different sort of ability to survive. The great redwoods grow large and straight. The banyan is sneaky. It simply grows anywhere and anyhow it possibly can— and as *twisted* as it can, I might add," the guide informed them. "Still, it is a valuable resource for other kinds of life here. A curious thing, eh?"

Jonny had to agree.

"Let us be off, then. Dusk comes soon."

"Time to camp?" said Jessie.

"Yes. We will camp at the place not only where the lights are the easiest to view but also where our little friend Ranjit—and others—have viewed the strange things they have reported."

"Oh, joy," said Jessie.

14

"WHERE'S DAD AND RACE?" SAID JONNY. "AND BANDIT?"

They had reached the place that was supposed to be their campsite. However, there was no sign of Jonny's father, Race, or Bandit—or the other Land Rover.

"Are you sure this is the place, Kailish?" said Jessie, obviously worried.

"Oh, yes, that I am. This was the place I circled on the map." He scratched his head. "They should have been here hours ago."

The sun was touching the horizon and spreading molten red and gold among the mountains in the distance. The air smelled of blossoms.

"We should try the radio," said Hadji.

They went to the car and attempted to reach the other half of their team. However, not only could they not reach Dr. Quest and Race, but there seemed to be some kind of interference.

"We cannot go looking for them," said Kailish. "It is dark. It is best that we should set up camp and hope they join us soon."

"Yeah. Maybe they discovered something exciting and went to investigate," said Jessie.

"And their radio doesn't work, either," said Jonny hopefully. Still, he was worried, too. "Yeah, that must be it."

He yawned and wished briefly that he'd had a nap that day, but he was too keyed up by the possibility of what might happen next to sleep right away.

The temperature had thankfully cooled a bit, and they made a fire by which to light their camp and heat their food—tins of spicy vegetarian food provided by Kailish. As soon as his friend Hadji had introduced him to it, Jonny had known that he liked Indian food, with its tang and its healthy emphasis on beans and vegetables, so this was no hardship.

As they finished their meal Kailish brought another item out of the Land Rover—an item that normally Jonny was not usually so happy to see.

It was a rifle.

Jonny knew they had agreed to take turns standing watch during the night, to keep an eye out not just for the lights or other unusual occurrences but also for predators. Even so, he felt uneasy.

"I'm qualified to use this," said Kailish. "And I am quite a good shot." He examined the bore and began to clean it. "It is just for protection, never fear. The ministry wouldn't let visitors as welcome as you inside the preserve without proper precautions!" He gestured back toward the car. "And of course we've got plenty of backup."

Jonny nodded.

The Land Rover was equipped with a radio. If they got into trouble, they could just call, and help would be on its way in whatever form the Indian government could provide it. That was, of course, presuming the interference lifted soon. However, since this was at the moment a low-priority mission for the Indian government, only one person—Kailish—and one vehicle had been assigned.

The government had also loaned them some equipment in addition to the items they'd brought themselves. Set up on mounts and tripods were spectrometers, radiation detectors, a camera with a telescopic lens, and other items they would need to record and analyze the phenomenon. It would do, though it was hardly high-tech.

More of a problem, though, was the computer the Indian government had loaned them.

Hadji looked down at the thing in his lap, puzzled. "What do you do with this thing—crank it?"

"No, no," said Kailish. "You just turn it on. Like so. However, if you wish to keep it on for a long time, you must plug it into this attachment, which provides it with power from one of the batteries in the Land Rover."

"Jonny, you are looking at an example of ancient Indian technology, produced long before I was born," said Hadji with a half smile.

"Gee, Hadji, looks like an old Zenith from the eighties to me," said Jessie.

"Oh, please," Hadji shot back. "I always enjoy pretending I am in touch with my ancestors." The backlit screen came on and displayed a menu.

79

"Oh, my, such choice!" Hadji exclaimed with a touch of sarcasm. "Well, I suppose if any calculations are necessary, this will work."

Kailish looked distraught. "I am so sorry, Master Hadji. You do not understand. Please do not be too disdainful of the technology at hand. This was all I could put together." He looked down at the ground and shook his head sadly. "You see, I, like you, am fascinated with mysteries, of which India has many. However, others at the ministry think I am foolish. They call me a crackpot." He gestured at the equipment. "This was all I could get. I am so sorry it's inadequate." The firelight flickered over his face, revealing his shame and embarrassment.

Jessie knelt beside him. "Oh, Kailish," she said, putting her arm around him, "this is just fine. You did a very good job. We'll be able to use this equipment with no problem."

Jessie looked over at the boys. Jonny could tell that Hadji felt as bad as he did. "Oh, yeah, this is *great,* Kailish," Jonny said reassuringly. "It'll do just fine."

"I was most rude," said Hadji. "Forgive me."

The smile returned to Kailish's face. "Thank you. I share your enthusiasm. I know that you have amazing technology in your hands back in your country." He touched his heart and his head. "But please believe me when I say that my intense desire to know the truth and my eagerness for knowledge are just as great as yours."

"So we *are* a team, then," said Jessie. "And we're going to discover exactly what's going on out there."

Jonny stepped away a short distance and looked out over the landscape. They were camped underneath some trees on a slight rise of earth. Some distance away, before the slopes of the mountains, was the lake area from which the lights arose inexplicably. The mountains beyond prevented access from the other side, and so the route in front of them was the only way to the lake.

In the starry sky above, a splendid moon hung, casting its silvery light over the magnificent ruins of the Forbidden City of Luxor, right by the lake.

It was much like the Fortress of Ranthambhore, only bigger and darker-seeming.

"Everything's all set up," Jonny said, returning to the group. "Who's got first watch?"

Jonny was dreaming about Hobbes the tiger chasing Calvin in a tangled QuestWorld cartoon background when a hand shook his shoulder.

"Jonny, wake up. Hurry. There's something going on down the slope," said Jessie.

Jonny got up. Excitement chased away his sleep. Kailish and Hadji were already up, looking expectant. Kailish had his gun by his side.

"Okay," said Jonny. "Let's have a look!"

He slung his backpack on and hopped down past the cooling coals of the fire.

He looked down.

"Yes, I *do see* something," he said. "But it's not near the lake. It's closer."

"I believe you are correct," said Kailish. "I do not think these are the lights that have been recorded. This could be one of the apparitions described by Ranjit and the other villagers."

Jonny grabbed his own personal camera from its pocket on his backpack. "Okay, I'm ready."

They hurried down the slope. Even as they made their way to the clearing, Jonny could see what Kailish meant.

Forming in the night air, in brilliant swirls of light, was the image of an ancient Indian god.

15

THE SWIRLING LIGHTS COLLECTED INTO SOMETHING FLOATING above the ground . . . something as big as a tree. Lights formed a body and legs—and many arms, all holding shiny swords. A demon-like face leered down at them with a forked tongue and eyes that blazed like atomic fires.

"Shiva the Destroyer!" said Kailish. He stood regarding the growing thing with awe.

Jonny took a moment to focus his camera and snapped off a quick series of shots.

The image of the huge god shimmered and vibrated. At one point he seemed almost like a streaming collection of Industrial Light and Magic special effects for some George Lucas production.

"Shiva the Destroyer," echoed Hadji, almost reverently.

Jessie stepped forward and waved. "Hi there, Shiva."

A voice blasted from the god. The long, deadly cutlasses in his hands glittered as he waved them in the air. "Be gone, mortals! Be gone from my province and desecrate it no more."

There was terror in Kailish's eyes, but he stood firm, holding his gun at the ready.

Hadji stepped forward. "Very impressive. I can see why the image strikes fear in my people."

Jonny slipped his camera back in its pocket. Then he knelt down and scooped up a rock. "Okay, Shiva. Sorry to be irreverent, but—" Jonny tossed the rock at the god.

The rock passed directly through the light, not slowing down at all. The god did not cease his frightening dance.

"I believe," said Hadji, "Shiva is beginning to sound more and more like Mrs. Thatcher."

Jonny nodded. "Come on, then. Shall we go and have a look?"

"Pay no attention to the funny little man behind the curtain!" said Jessie.

"What?" said Kailish.

"Just a quote from *The Wizard of Oz*. Don't worry, Kailish. The thing looks so fierce because it's really so harmless. Come and have a look."

Kailish nodded and accompanied them, but nonetheless he kept a firm grip on his firearm.

Jonny, Hadji, and Jessie all had flashlights, which they played on the ground surrounding the apparition.

Hadji looked over at Jonny. "You are clearly thinking what I'm thinking. . . ."

"Yes," said Jonny.

Jessie kept her flashlight moving, ignoring the bizarre antics of the dancing Indian god. "Over there in the bushes, maybe?"

"Good call. It seems we don't need any kind of special detectors for this one," said Jonny.

"Just the old schnozola," said Jessie. "And boy, do I smell something fishy."

"Not more crocodiles, I most sincerely hope," said Kailish.

Despite the looming terror of the flashing swords that flailed above them, Jonny and company walked forward. To either side of the thirty-foot-high image was a large bush. Jonny walked up to the closest one and pulled back the branches while Hadji directed his flashlight down through the foliage.

"Well, what do you know," said Jessie.

Hidden in the bush was a strange-looking device consisting of metal panels, glass lenses, and several control knobs. From the lenses streams of light shot out in a rainbow of colors, forming the magnificent creation dancing above them.

"Yep," said Jonny. "Just as I thought."

"A hologram," said Jessie.

Hadji turned to Kailish. "Any guess as to who is responsible for this?" There was a challenging tone in his voice.

"What? Surely you don't think it's the Indian ministry," Kailish gasped. "Look at this technology! We could never afford anything like it."

Hadji nodded. "I did not think so, but I had to ask nonetheless."

Jonny reached down and twisted a couple of the knobs.

The three-dimensional image flickered, changed

colors, and then was sucked back into the darkness of the night.

"So what's something like this doing in the middle of a nature preserve?" said Jonny.

"It's meant to deter the curious," said Hadji.

"And clearly that's just what it's been very successful at—keeping people away from a certain area," said Jessie.

"The area that contains the source of the lights!" said Kailish.

"Yes. And I have a hunch I know who put it here," Jonny said grimly.

"Hyde-Pierce?"

"Precisely."

"But why?"

"I suppose we'll know more about that just as soon as we discover what the true source of the phenomenon is," said Jonny. "Right now what we need is more clues. Jessie and Hadji, why don't you tinker with this thing here? Kailish, you hold a flashlight. Be careful that the device isn't booby-trapped."

"What about you?" Jessie asked.

"There's some forest over there, and from Ranjit's description, that's closer to where he actually saw *his* bogeyman. I'm going to go over and see if I can turn up another machine. If I'm gone longer than five or six minutes, call for me."

"Right. It's not very far," said Kailish. "And shout if you find something. I feel very bad that I have no walkie-talkies."

"Don't worry. We'll survive," said Jonny, and struck off, the beam of his flashlight bobbing off tree trunks and fronds. He followed a makeshift path into a clearing and flashed the beam around.

He sighed. Nothing much there . . . and if there was anything, it was buried too deeply in the darkness for him to see. He should go back, he thought, and turned.

Standing in front of him was a tiger.

Jonny jerked back. Then he halted himself.

It certainly didn't look real.

It seemed somehow elevated in the air, and it uttered absolutely no sound.

Nor was there any smell to it, and Kailish had assured him that a musky smell—the smell of a meat-eater—was one of the principal signs that a tiger was in the vicinity.

"Right," he said challengingly, flashing his light toward the tiger. "It's probably just you, Hyde-Pierce, trying to scare us off. If the image of Shiva doesn't work, you might as well try something scary from the natural world. Hyde-Pierce, do you hear me? I know you must have some kind of audio on your devices."

The tiger roared, then reached a huge paw forward and knocked the flashlight from Jonny's hand. It spun off to the edge of the glade and landed with the beam pointing back into the clearing, giving a ghostly glow to the place as the tiger prepared to charge Jonny.

"Uh-oh," muttered Jonny.

16

THE TIGER GROWLED.

It was the kind of growl meant to inspire fear in lesser creatures, and it worked in Jonny.

It *still* didn't smell, but now he could see that its unearthliness had been as illusion. Jonny's knees seemed to give out from under him.

Intimidation, some part of Jonny's brain recalled. *That's part of the tiger's stock in trade. Scare the prey, then take it down and have a lip-smacking treat.*

This particular tiger was a magnificent example of the breed, with beautiful stripes and long whiskers. Long fangs glimmered with saliva in the light from the fallen flashlight.

The enormous cat roared, preparing for its charge.

On the forest floor before him, Jonny saw a piece of wood. It was a pitiful weapon, but it was better than nothing.

He bent slowly, picked it up, and held it up before the tiger.

The tiger sprang. Simultaneously Jonny screamed,

"Help!" Then he tossed the stick directly up into the air and hurled himself off to the side as hard as he could.

The tiger's terrible claws slashed forward, right at the stick, missing Jonny by mere inches. The incredible strength of its springing attack carried it yards past Jonny, and it crashed into a tangle of foliage.

Were he one of the antelopes they had seen earlier that day, Jonny reflected briefly, he would have the speed to sprint cleanly away. That was why a tiger had to succeed on the first try. But Jonny knew he didn't have that kind of speed, Quest Team sneakers on or not.

Still, he couldn't do anything else but try. Without even a pause for breath, he sprinted back toward the camp.

Behind him came a roar of frustration and then another of determination.

Jonny thought he heard the sound of the creature chasing him through the brush. He strained his body to the utmost, pushing for every last bit of speed he could muster. He hurtled onward, fancying that he could feel the tiger's hot breath on the back of his neck.

Run, man, he urged himself. *Run.*

Finally he saw the others up ahead. Hadji held a flashlight. Kailish held his rifle.

"It's a tiger!" yelled Jonny.

There was a sudden fierce barking, and a dog sprang into the tiger's path.

Jonny veered off slightly and turned around. "Bandit! What are you doing here?"

The dog barked even louder, making short, violent lunges toward the tiger, each time pulling away at the last moment.

The tiger seemed absolutely stunned that a creature so small would have the nerve to stand in its way. Bandit had done his job, but Jonny could see that it wouldn't be long before the tiger got sick of this little animal and batted him away with its powerful claws.

Jonny reached down, grabbed the bulldog, clasped him firmly against his chest, and started running again.

The tiger still seemed stunned by this turn of events and did not react with another lunge, giving Jonny valuable time. As he ran he saw Hadji's light streaking through the forest, and he noticed Kailish lifting his gun.

"Don't—" began Jonny.

Kailish fired.

The crack of a rifle was always much louder than Jonny ever recalled it being. Puffing, he turned around to see the tiger's fate.

It stood there in the light, motionless but still quite alive and defiant. It had not been hurt at all, Jonny realized.

"I will not shoot the tiger unless I absolutely must," said Kailish. "Stay very still now . . . its race still remembers the gun."

The tiger snarled and crouched close to the ground, ready to pounce.

"It looks like that attack behavior is something else the tigers haven't forgotten," Hadji murmured.

"Stand your ground. I will shoot if I must," said

Kailish. He no longer seemed a self-conscious fumbler, but a strong and determined man.

Jonny's heart ached at the possibility of seeing such a beautiful animal killed. *Don't come, tiger,* he thought, still breathing heavily.

The tiger didn't seem to be able to read minds, though, and it tensed its muscles, ready to spring. Just as it was about to pounce, however, something appeared between it and the humans—something huge and flashing.

Sword blades whirled, and a mighty voice thundered, "Be gone, mortals!"

The tiger was there one moment, and the next it was simply *gone*.

The hologram of Shiva lingered for a few moments for good measure, and then disappeared.

Jonny turned around, breathed a sigh of great relief, and waved back toward where Jessie stood by the machine.

"I see you mastered the controls," he said.

"Yes. And Shiva and I are going to go on tour. Care to make an investment in our show?" replied Jessie in a cocky voice.

"Sure. And oh, yeah—thanks, Jess," said Jonny.

"And I thank you as well," said Kailish. "It would have been a very hard thing indeed to live with myself after shooting that tiger."

"I imagine that the tiger also might have had a hard time living with himself if you'd shot him," Hadji added. He turned. "Bandit, where are Race and Dr. Quest?"

The little dog jumped from Jonny's arms to the

ground, barked, and ran around in circles. He looked baffled and seriously upset. As Jonny bent over to examine him, he could see that the dog had picked up a lot of burrs and tiny twigs in his short fur. He'd obviously traveled a long way.

"How did you find us, boy?"

Bandit barked. He sounded as though he were saying, *It wasn't easy. And it sure was dangerous.*

Hadji stepped to Jonny's side. "Your father and Race must be in trouble. And yet there is not much we can do at night. We shall have to wait until we can send a radio message . . . or until dawn, when we can look for them."

They went back to the hologram machine. "Hadji and I have been looking at its insides," said Jessie. "But we still can't get into this area here."

"I believe there are appropriate tools among the supplies I have just unpacked from the Land Rover," said Kailish. "Just a moment. I will go and get them. Jonny, are you well enough to come and help me?"

"Sure. I could use a drink of water anyway."

Bandit barked.

"Sounds like Bandit wants one, too . . . and something to eat!"

"Two cups of cool water, coming up," said Kailish. "And some dinner for your brave dog as well. Come, my lad. The evening is taking some interesting twists and turns."

I just hope those twists and turns lead us to an answer to this puzzle, thought Jonny. *And that we stay in one piece.*

92

"I am sorry," said Kailish as they walked toward where the food supplies were stored. "I did not think a tiger would venture so close to an encampment. There have been virtually no man-eaters in this area for a very long time."

"Yeah, well, I think he was just pissed off in general. I think it's not just people who get spooked around here."

"Ah, yes. No doubt. In fact, I was rather thinking that—"

Kailish was interrupted by the sound of the Land Rover's engine starting.

"What—?" he said, bewildered.

The lights of the vehicle sprang on. The engine revved, and the vehicle started heading straight for them.

17

"THERE'S NO ONE AT THE WHEEL!" CRIED KAILISH, STUNNED. He seemed fixed in place, held fast by the headlights of the Land Rover as it barreled toward them.

True, thought Jonny. *But that doesn't mean the thing can't run us over.* With swift reflexes, he grabbed their guide by his jacket and pulled hard.

Bandit barked once and then got out of the way as well.

They dodged the Land Rover, avoiding its hard metal grille and ridged tires by just a very little bit. As it whizzed by, the spinning wheels splattered them with dirt.

At first Jonny thought for sure that the driverless vehicle would whirl around, gun its engine, and make another go at them.

However, it did not. Instead it continued on in the direction it was going and was soon swallowed up by the night.

Hadji, who had seen the vehicle careening into the brush, chased it for a few seconds, but when it became apparent that he would never reach the speeding Land

Rover, he turned around. "What's going on?" he said as he made his way over to Jonny and Kailish.

"I think one of your Indian gods has hijacked our car!" said Jonny.

"Actually, from the level of technology displayed by that hologram device over there," said Jessie, coming over and helping Kailish up, "I'd say it's more likely that the car was wired so that it could be operated by remote control. Somebody wanted us to get stranded out here in the middle of the night."

"I wonder who that could possibly be," said Jonny grimly.

"You still think that Dr. Hyde-Pierce is involved with all this?" said Kailish.

"I think he's our man, yeah. Him and his cockney sidekick. We're not dealing with technological yahoos, you know."

"Oh, dear. How unfortunate . . . and the radio and cellular phone are in the car," said Kailish. "Well, when I am not heard from in a report later on this evening, help will be dispatched . . . I hope."

"It wasn't as though the radio was working, anyway." Jessie sighed. "Oh, well. We still have the equipment. We can still make observations."

"Yes," said Hadji. "And when Jessie and I were looking at the interior of that hologram device, I got an idea. . . ."

The group was surrounded by equipment, wires, and parts from the dismantled hologram machine. Hadji tinkered with one final adjustment, using the few tools he had, than stood back and regarded his handiwork by the light of a lamp powered by a small generator they'd taken from the Land Rover before it had turned on them.

"Yes, I believe this will provide the kind of transmission needed," he said.

"I am sorry," said Kailish, "but I do not understand. If you will please explain what you are doing here . . . "

"May I?" said Jessie, looking at Hadji. Both she and Jonny had contributed to this effort; considering the limited equipment at hand, Jonny thought, they had really done a very good job indeed.

"Certainly," said Hadji. "I will just ready the transmitter."

"You see," Jessie explained to Kailish, "from the information we received earlier, we speculated that the lights emanating from the lake were just an aftereffect of another process, one that might involve a crystal— or a diamond."

"And crystals can also be used to construct a kind of radio," Jonny put in. "In fact, the earliest radios used crystals."

"Ah, I begin to see," said Kailish.

"Yes," Jonny confirmed. "And what Hadji has done is to use parts of the hologram machine to construct another device that will emit radio waves—and, we hope, trigger the other unit, the one producing the mysterious lights."

Hadji smiled. "That's right. The apparatus responsible for the lights may be a sort of device that produces a large variety of electromagnetic radiation—not just visible light but also radio waves, ultraviolet radiation, X rays, and gamma rays. We're getting evidence that *all* of those are present here." He shrugged and tapped the equipment he'd assembled. "At the very worst we have a radio with which we can signal for help."

"Yes," said Jonny. "Right now, though, we'd better just keep things quiet. We don't know who'll be listening in, so we shouldn't broadcast any messages just yet."

"Indeed. All we'll do is broadcast at the frequencies suggested by the data that you gave us." Hadji gave Kailish a smile. "And by the way, your computer did turn out to be quite helpful in the process. Please forgive me my technological snobbery."

"Oh, never mind that," said Kailish eagerly. "Please, let us see what happens with your splendid idea."

"Okay, Jonny?" said Hadji.

"Let's give it a try, Hadj," said Jonny, looking down at the large mess of wires, resistors, and transistors. "I've got it on the bandwidth and frequencies we talked about earlier."

"Good. Here we go!" Hadji flipped a switch.

The power hummed, and lights glowed within the heap of equipment. A small speaker squealed with static, then whooped and warbled as Jonny spun the knobs slowly and carefully.

"The first range of frequencies has been covered now," said Hadji. "Anything going on out there?"

Jonny looked up.

The moon was behind a cloud, but the vague outlines of the mountains could still be seen above the soft gleam of the lake and the hulking ruins of the Forbidden City of Luxor. That was all—no mysterious lights.

"Nope. You want to try a wider frequency range?"

"Sure. Let's do it."

Jonny twiddled the knob back and forth slowly. Suddenly they heard a high, keening noise.

"Stop it there," said Hadji. "That's something."

"Yeah, maybe a punk rock station from Bombay or something," Jessie joked.

"Ha, ha," said Jonny. "What we need is a little moral support. Let's keep it here for a minute, Hadji. It's only slightly beyond the parameters you calculated."

"Yes, indeed. What do we have to lose?"

They watched the horizon expectantly, but nothing happened.

Jonny's stomach fell with disappointment. *Maybe,* he thought dispiritedly, *we should just bite the bullet and figure out how to use this radio to call for some help, and then—*

"Jonny," said Jessie. "Look!"

Jonny looked up.

Bandit woofed with excitement.

Lights were fountaining up from the lake, bathing the Forbidden City of Luxor in an eerie glow.

18

THESE WERE NO ORDINARY LIGHTS.

They fountained up like sprays of thick laser beams streaming into the air.

A bank of clouds had sailed low across the sky. The lights stabbed into these clouds, creating layers of soft color.

Then the lights began to twirl like some New Age carousel.

"I think," said Jonny unnecessarily, "that's them."

"And they aren't that far away!" Jessie raised her binoculars to her eyes. "I can see something!" she said. "I can see what the lights are emerging from! Here, Jonny. Have a look."

Jonny took the glasses and looked into them. He had to refocus slightly, but then he could see what Jessie was talking about.

A large metal hump had risen up from the lake, near the shore. It was big enough that its rim now touched the fronds of the plants at the edge of the lake.

"You're right," said Jonny. "It's maybe a mile or a

mile and a half away. But without a boat, you have to go through the Forbidden City."

Hadji was busy clicking off photos. Jonny looked at the equipment, then looked at Kailish standing there with awe on his face. Jessie seemed excited and eager.

"Kailish, we should go down there. Someone should stay up here, though, and monitor Hadji's device. I'm afraid that if something goes wrong with it, whatever that metal thing is will sink back underneath the lake."

Kailish blinked. "What—me? You will go down there, and I should stay here?"

"You've never dealt with this kind of situation before," said Jonny. "We have."

"I see. Well, I shall not argue with you. The mystery must be solved, and I must play my part. That is why you are here." He braced himself manfully, clearly sad that he wasn't going to be able to take part in this final part of the exploration. "Very well. But hurry. And please . . . take my rifle."

"No," said Jonny. "That won't be necessary. You keep the rifle, Kailish." He turned to the rest of the team. "Come on, guys. Let's go and have a look at this thing!"

Bandit barked excitedly.

The Forbidden City of Luxor was a web of shadows below the bright Indian moon. Its buildings were ancient and crumbling. There were toppled towers and fallen minarets, and there were buildings like the ones in the Fortress of Ranthambhore, only many were bigger—hulking phantoms of a long-ago age. It smelled of decay and old things, and there was a taste of chill in the air. The Quest Team made its way through the rubble and the vegetation-choked streets and alleys.

Coo-coo-caw! A plaintive cry came from one of the distant buildings. *Coo-coo-coo-caw!*

"What was that?" said Jonny. He wasn't scared so much as cautious. He shone his flashlight into the shadows. It barely illuminated anything.

"Hard to say," said Hadji. "Let's just get through this place and to the lake. It's not our job to explore the city."

"Hadji's right," Jessie added. "Other people can deal with this place. Our job is what's sitting out there in that lake."

Bandit ran ahead of them suddenly, barking.

"Bandit!" said Jessie. "Bandit, don't go anywhere."

The dog ignored her and continued running up to one of the bigger buildings. He stopped in front of a huge archway with carved pictures of gods and men. Any wooden doors that had been there had long since rotted away.

Inside was inky darkness—darkness that seemed to *move,* like something alive. Jonny felt a cold sensation creep along his spine.

Bandit ran back and forth just outside the doorway into this world of darkness and yipped. Turning back toward the rest of the Quest Team, he let out another excited bark.

"Bandit smells something in there," said Jessie.

"Yes, but what?" said Hadji. "Doubtless there are many dangerous things that live in these buildings. Perhaps we should leave them be and get on with our task."

Jonny was inclined to agree. He shone his light on the dog and was about to sternly order Bandit to come back from the entrance when he saw a strange expression on the dog's face, a kind of desperate pleading.

Jonny knew that Bandit was an extremely intelligent dog, and he was seldom wrong. Clearly he felt that there was something important inside that building . . . something that was worth the danger of entering.

"No," said Jonny to the others. "Wait a minute. Bandit seems determined. Maybe we'd better check this out."

"I'm not so sure," said Hadji.

"It won't take more than a minute," said Jonny. "If you two want to stay out here, that's okay. But I'm going to take Bandit in and see what he wants me to see in there."

Bandit yapped, spinning around in circles with excitement at this decision.

"Okay, boy," said Jonny as he stepped forward to join the dog. "Just don't go charging ahead. Stay with me."

Bandit barked agreement.

Jessie and Hadji came over to join them. "So let's go, Bandit," Jessie said. "Show us what you want us to see."

They followed the dog into the building.

102

The archway opened out into a courtyard, the walls of which were covered with vines and creepers. Chittering noises could be heard coming from the foliage.

"Monkeys?" said Jessie hopefully.

"Yes," said Hadji. "And that is a good sign. If there was something really dangerous back here, monkeys certainly wouldn't hang around."

"Let's hope so," said Jessie. "I don't see any other doors, though."

Jonny flashed his light across the vegetation. He couldn't see anything, either. However, Bandit dashed forward toward a cluster of shadows and stood there, as though alertly pointing the way.

Sure enough, when they got up to where the dog was, they could see a narrow doorway. Cautiously they entered. Jonny found himself in a small passageway. Old sculptures were nestled in niches carved into the walls.

The hallway was not very long, and it opened up into another, larger courtyard. Across the flagstoned area, a light flickered.

"What is that?" said Jonny, alarmed.

"Looks like a torch to me," said Jessie. "Any thoughts, Hadji?"

"I would urge caution—but we must check this out!"

Jonny couldn't disagree. This seemed like a distraction from their main task, yes, but clearly Bandit was right—there was something important here.

The orange-red light flickered again. It appeared to

be guttering in some phantom breeze. As he got closer Jonny could see that the glow was coming from a room of some sort. He stepped up to the door and saw that the light was indeed from a torch, which was stuck in a sconce on the wall.

Below, illuminated by the torchlight, were two forms, tied up and huddled together in a corner.

"Dad!" said Jonny. "Race!"

The others entered as well. The room smelled of damp and age and the kerosene-soaked torch—and something else.

Jessie ran over to untie the adults.

Bandit barked, then growled and backed up, the fur on the back of his neck rising.

From the shadows, a form prowled forward, a deeper growl in its throat.

Hadji gasped and backed away. "Oh, no—it's Mrs. Thatcher."

Jonny looked around. "Dr. Hyde-Pierce, Higgins Doodle . . . are you here?"

"The tiger's not talking. They must not be here," said Jessie. "The tiger's guarding Dad and Dr. Quest . . . "

"And this is a trap," finished Jonny.

The tiger growled again, opening its mouth and showing huge fangs.

"Could be," Hadji said. "But it's not attacking. Wait a minute." The Indian boy stepped forward.

"Hadji!" cried Jessie.

"Shhh!" whispered Hadji. "Show no fear!" He stepped forward slowly, eyes locked with the tiger's. He crept ahead and then lowered himself to his hands and knees until his face was level with the large beast's. All the tiger had to do was make one slash of its mighty claws and that would have been it for Hadji.

However, if anything, the huge cat seemed to calm down as it stared into the boy's eyes. For a tense moment the two were totally motionless. Then Hadji reached out and put his hand against the tiger's head. He spoke to it in a low tone.

The tiger opened its mouth. It moved its head toward Hadji—

And then a large tongue emerged and licked Hadji's face.

Hadji rubbed behind the tiger's ears and turned back to the others. "We are bonded now. I have told her not to fear us . . . and not to hurt us."

"Hadji," said Jonny, "how—"

"The practice of yogin has many facets. One branch of it draws on ancient principles of man and beast. I merely tapped into those." He looked at the tiger and added, "Mrs. Thatcher is not a man-killer, and she is accustomed to humans. However, I do not think she likes her current masters much."

"That's not surprising!" said Jessie. "Good job, Hadji. Jonny, help me with Dad and Dr. Quest."

Jonny took out his utility knife. In a couple of minutes Dr. Quest and Race were untied. However, they were still unconscious. Once free of their bonds, they simply slumped back onto the floor.

"Drugged," said Jonny.

"Their pulses are normal," said Jessie. "They'll be

105

okay. But we can't carry them with us. Maybe someone should stay with them."

"I volunteer," said Hadji. "Mrs. Thatcher and I are friends now—she will help as well."

"Okay. We'll come back for you as soon as possible," said Jonny. "Bandit, you come along too. Just in case Mrs. Thatcher is a little bit hungry."

Bandit whined nervously and followed them back out into the city.

By the time they got to the edge of the lake, the lights were slowly dying out.

However, the thing that had risen up from the lake was still very much there.

Bandit yapped with excitement.

"It's some kind of ship," Jonny surmised.

"A flying saucer?" asked Jessie.

"No. It seems to be somewhat lozenge-shaped," said Jonny.

"Whatever else it is, it's big."

It looked like an alien submarine rising up out of the water, gray and mottled. Jagged, toothlike edges ridged the top and were clear evidence of how the thing had cut its way out of its hiding place in the silt at the bottom of the lake.

At the very apex of these teeth there seemed to be some kind of platform.

And on the top of this platform, set like a bit of jewelry in an intricate array of metalwork, was the biggest crystal that Jonny had ever seen.

"A diamond?" said Jessie, stunned. She stopped in the fronds ridging the lake.

"I'm not sure a diamond can *get* that big," said Jonny. "But it's some kind of crystal, all right."

"I wonder if it's even from this world," said Jessie, adjusting her camera lens and taking another quick series of pictures.

"That's what we have to find out," said Jonny. "Come on. The lights seem to be going off. We'd better get a closer look. It might go down at any time."

Jonny, Jessie, and Bandit started approaching the ship that had risen from the lake.

Suddenly another light stabbed out of the sky.

Then came the roaring *chop-chop* of rotor blades. The cone of light swept along the ground, finally fixing on the two teenagers.

"Think they're ministry agents, come looking for us because Kailish couldn't check in?" said Jessie hopefully.

"I sure hope so," said Jonny.

Bandit barked, but the sound was drowned out by the roar of the helicopter rotors.

It was a smallish helicopter, not the large government type that Jonny had expected.

An amplified voice thundered down. "Please! Stay exactly where you are!"

The helicopter's light picked out a suitable landing spot, and then the copter dipped down and landed.

Two men jumped off the helicopter. Both carried guns.

And the guns were pointed directly at Jonny and Jessie.

19

"GOOD EVENING, MASTER QUEST. QUEST! OH, HOW APPROPRIATE is that name, it would seem," snapped a tart British voice.

Jonny recognized it.

"Dr. Hyde-Pierce. Where did you get that helicopter?"

"A little cash in the right place generally gets me exactly what I need, even in primitive, nasty countries like this," said Hyde-Pierce in an arch, superior voice.

"Well, you would certainly seem to have a Land Rover now," said Jessie.

"The point was not to procure a Land Rover so much as to deprive you of one." Hyde-Pierce stepped out into the faint light, and now they could see him as more than just a silhouette holding a handgun. He looked over at the huge outline of the vessel in the water. "While my tactics to keep you away seem to have been of no use, I dare say we should not even have bothered, for you have found something that we have been looking for a few weeks. Isn't that so, Higgins?"

Higgins Doodle stepped into the light as well. He also held a handgun. "That's right. 'Ow'd you do it, then?"

Jessie put her hands on her hips. "Maybe we just asked nicely," she snapped.

"Where are your other friends?" asked Hyde-Pierce.

"Safely back at camp," said Jonny, deciding it was better not to tell them that Hadji was with Dr. Quest and Race. He also thought he'd better change the subject. "I'm confused. We don't know what that vessel is or why you want it."

"Haven't figured it out, then, have you?" said Hyde-Pierce.

"We might make some wild guesses, but as long as you know," said Jonny, "you might as well tell us quickly. That thing can go back down as fast as it came up. And to tell you the truth, I'm very curious to take a closer look."

"Yes," said Hyde-Pierce. "As are we all. Higgins, what do you think?"

"Well, guv'nor, they're smart. That could be good, and that could be bad." He frowned at Jonny. "'Ow'd you get it to come up in the first place?"

"A little technological wizardry," replied Jonny.

"How, exactly?" asked Hyde-Pierce. "You'll get definite points for cooperation."

Jonny outlined the basic procedure for him.

Even in the darkness, Hyde-Pierce's eyes seemed to glow with appreciation. "Very clever. Very clever indeed. Why didn't I think of that, Doodle?"

"You would have soon enough, sir, I'll warrant."

Hyde-Pierce preened, some of his pride having returned. "Yes, yes. Of course I would have . . . thank you, Higgins. Shall we wander over and have a look at that thing now? Looks to be quite a catch—rather a treat for us scientists, eh?" He gestured with his gun.

The moon shone through a break in the clouds as they walked along the beach toward the mysterious object.

"Why are you doing this, Hyde-Pierce?" asked Jonny.

"Raise those hands a tad higher, and I'll tell you, lad."

"Guv'nor!" protested Doodle.

The two men engaged in some fierce whispering. Jonny was able to pick up only a part of their conversation, but what he heard gave him a chill: ". . . can't have them knowing about this," said Doodle. Hyde-Pierce replied in a low voice, and all Jonny could hear was ". . . not going to last long. Might as well tell them."

Doodle seemed to like this well enough, because he quieted down.

"Science is, of course, quite important," continued Hyde-Pierce in a normal tone. "But equally important is the technology it spawns. That, my friends, is the secret to my success. You see, the governments of this world have far more money than the ridiculous little puffed-up universities or research institutes. If you bring them something they want, they will heap riches upon you."

"What a lot of governments want are high-tech

weapons," Jessie said. "So much for pure scientific inquiry. You just want to sell this to the highest bidder."

"I'm confused," said Jonny. "How do you know it's a weapon? It would appear to be a stranded vessel from another world."

"Oh, and the secrets it holds will be of great value to the country that can pay for them," said Hyde-Pierce. "Of course, they need a top-notch scientist to interpret it all. And as for weapons, well, any culture that can produce light like this—coherent light, the stuff of lasers—can surely create . . . oh, dear. What did they call them in that silly science-fiction film we saw the other day, Higgins?"

"Death rays, guv'nor."

"Oh, the language! Shakespeare himself would have been delighted." Hyde-Pierce gestured toward the ship. "At the very least, people, what we have here is something that can be turned into a death ray, hmmm? But let us go and see." They had reached the edge of the lake. Hyde-Pierce waggled his gun. "Please. You first."

Jonny understood now. Hyde-Pierce not only wanted them to help him get inside the ship, but he also wanted them to go first in case there were any traps.

"You're so kind." Jonny turned to Jessie. "So what do you think, Jess? Something from another planet— or a lost ship from a secret government program somewhere?"

"Only time will tell," said Jessie.

111

Bandit woofed.

Running up the side of the vessel was a series of neat steplike cuts that could easily serve as stairs. These led right up to the crystal that was the source of the lights, which had almost completely died out by now.

"Up we go, then," said Doodle, gesturing with his gun. "Don't dawdle."

Jonny went first. His mind worked furiously.

This was not a good situation, and they would just have to play it by ear. Their one card in the hole now was Kailish, but Jonny wondered if Kailish was even aware of what was going on down by the lake.

Surely he'd have seen the helicopter. But then, wouldn't Kailish think that it could be help from the ministry, as Jonny and Jessie had? And hadn't they instructed Kailish to remain behind and keep the radio running and on that frequency so that the ship wouldn't resubmerge itself under the lake?

No, this was not a good situation at all.

They went up the steps cautiously. Jessie shot her light forward. The huge crystal was pulsing softly with faint light.

Up ahead, just short of it, was a metal hatch of some sort.

"What makes you think we can get in?" said Jessie.

"That's just something that we have to try, now, isn't it, people?" said Hyde-Pierce. "You're the clever ones. Solve the puzzle!"

The steps led to a flat landing area, and Jessie

walked across it toward the hatch. "I don't know," she muttered. "Why should it let *us* in?"

"Because you're such *good* people," said Doodle sarcastically.

Jessie kicked the hatch.

"'Ere, have a care, girl," Doodle said, sounding alarmed. "Somethin' might blow!"

"Well, I haven't a clue how to get in," she sniffed.

"Ah, and that is where I come in. I have anticipated this possibility," said Dr. Hyde-Pierce. "I am not so slow-witted myself, you see." He brought out a radio device with an antenna. "I have often wondered about the details of alien technology. However, even if this is an alien vessel, your little homemade radio device has proven what I have always known must be true—all technology operates under the same basic principles, whether it is from Earth or Alpha Centauri. I believe I need only diddle with the frequencies—eh, Higgins?"

"That's right, guv'nor. You just do that now. I'll keep me eye on these tricky youngsters." He raised his gun to make sure that Jonny and Jessie saw that it was still trained on them.

The device in Hyde-Pierce's hands twittered and bleeped.

Suddenly something deep in the vessel on which they stood responded. A circle of lights around the hatch twinkled.

Bandit barked and backed away. Then the dog turned and raced away into the dark.

Doodle lifted his gun to fire at Bandit, but Hyde-

Pierce stopped him. "Don't waste ammunition. The jungle will get the blasted animal. We've got more important things concerning us." He pointed to the hatch.

With a sound not unlike that of a hydraulic lift, the door of what might have been an alien spaceship opened.

20

SOFT, STRANGE LIGHTS GLIMMERED FROM WITHIN.

An ancient odor of dust and oil and strange spices wafted up from the interior of the vessel.

Hyde-Pierce chortled with joy. He peered down. "Well, well, well—it looks to be a room full of interesting items. And how considerate—there appears to be a ladder that descends into it. Jonny, why don't you and your friend Jessie go first? We would very much like to see just how friendly the initial steps are."

Jonny nodded. He felt a twinge of fear but suppressed it. He looked down. Sure enough, there was a ladder. It looked like many other ladders he'd seen, one metal rung after another. Only these rungs seemed rather widely spaced.

He started letting himself down.

Well, if there are any traps down here, he thought, *I'll know about them soon.*

When he'd gone down two rungs, Hyde-Pierce called out to him, "Stop right there, Quest."

Jonny looked up. He could see Hyde-Pierce

leering over toward Jessie. "I've changed my mind. Best not to let those two down there together, eh, Higgins?"

Doodle chuckled. "That's right, guv'nor."

"I'll follow you, Quest. And have a care not to pull any tricks. Not only do I have this gun, but I also have training in the martial arts. Besides, I'm sure that if you pull something, Higgins will have no qualms about ventilating your friend."

"Trigger finger's getting awfully twitchy, it is," said Doodle with a malevolent chuckle.

Jonny continued stepping down into the softly lit interior of the strange ship. He looked up briefly and saw Hyde-Pierce following him.

Jonny jumped down the last few rungs to the floor. It was metal as well, and the sound of his feet hitting it echoed through the chamber.

The room was round, with lights blinking softly around the perimeter. The control panels were illuminated also, and Jonny saw the letters of an alphabet he knew was not from this planet. The buttons on the control panels were various kinds of geometric shapes. As far as Jonny knew, those shapes had never been used on ships of any Earth civilization.

"Looks alien to me," said Jonny.

Hyde-Pierce stepped from the last rung of the ladder to the floor, still gripping the side of the ladder. He peered about, a sly smile curling his lips. "What did you expect—a Lemurian canoe? Of course it's an alien vessel! You couldn't decide that from the data that had already been presented to you?"

116

"We didn't have much data before we got here," Jonny replied.

"Well, it makes no difference," said Hyde-Pierce. "In any event, it's *my* alien ship now. All we need do is unlock its various secrets."

"Something must be wrong with it." Jonny pulled out his flashlight and swung its beam across the other end of the chamber. The beam hit a few structures that could be seats. Upon these seats were piles of dark dust.

"The former crew, stuck inside for thousands and thousands of years?" said Jonny. "Imagine—what were once living beings have decomposed to *that*."

"I wonder what went wrong." Hyde-Pierce pointed toward an area. "Could you kindly direct your light yonder?"

Jonny did so. There, instead of the usual control panels, was a blackened, burned hole. From this protruded various pieces of thick cable. The flexible housing of the cable had been torn open, exposing bare wires.

"Looks like some sort of accident," Jonny said, so caught up in the excitement of this amazing discovery that he almost forgot that there was a gun trained on him. "And I bet that's why this thing has been rising up periodically from its hiding place. Its circuits must have somehow awakened and are know repairing themselves. And those lights—maybe they served as some kind of beacon," he mused.

"Ah, yes—a signal for help," said Hyde-Pierce. "I must admit that the thought occurred to me as well."

"You may not have wonderful ethics, but there's nothing wrong with your intelligence, Doctor." Jonny drifted over to the blackened hole and looked at the wires that were sticking out. They seemed to be two pieces of a single cable that had somehow snapped or been torn apart. As he studied the array, a thought occurred to him.

In the meantime, Hyde-Pierce was saying, "Well, thank you, Jonny. Perhaps if my other colleagues had been more appreciative of me, those ethics might have been different. . . ." He thought about that a moment, then shook his head. "No, probably not." Swiveling his head, he called up the ladder. "Higgins!"

"Yes, guv'nor?"

"Would you be so kind as to hand down my special analysis mechanism and the tool kit? Perhaps we will be able to take total control of this ship."

"Right, guv'nor."

While Hyde-Pierce was talking, Jonny took advantage of his inattention. He stepped forward and took one of the cable sections in his hand. It was stiff and heavy, but he didn't lift weights for nothing. Then he pulled the other end of the cable around so that the wires from the two pieces of cable were touching.

A spark snapped. Then came an explosion and a blinding light. The force of it knocked Jonny back against the other wall.

21

JONNY STRUGGLED TO REMAIN CONSCIOUS, BUT IT WASN'T EASY.
The blast of light still seemed to be repeating itself in
strange and streaming patterns across the back of his
eyes. Reaching out blindly, he touched one of the odd
chairs and pulled himself up.

Then he noticed that the ship was vibrating.

Where the control panels before had merely been
faintly illuminated, now they were alive with brightly
flashing lights.

The ship had come alive!

Hyde-Pierce had lost his balance as a result of the
explosion. He put a hand on the ladder to steady
himself. "You idiot!" he cried. "What have you
done?"

"Just trying to understand—"

"Nonsense! You're trying to *ruin* me!" snarled
Hyde-Pierce. "I should have shot you immediately. But
I'll take care of that little matter right now!" Grimacing,
Hyde-Pierce raised his pistol.

Desperately Jonny cast about for a place to jump

119

away from the impending bullet, but there was nowhere to run.

His eyes gleeful, Hyde-Pierce started to laugh. He straightened his gun arm—

"Oof!" cried a voice above.

Suddenly Doodle dropped headfirst from the hatchway above, landing directly on Hyde-Pierce. They both went down in a confused tangle of arms and legs and guns, cursing and scrabbling amid the blinking confusion.

"Jonny!" called Jessie from above. "Get out of there right now. Something's going to happen!"

"No kidding!" Jonny launched himself at the ladder. He grabbed it halfway up and climbed desperately the rest of the way to the hatch.

"Higgins, you idiot! You'll blow everything. Get off me," cried the scientist.

"I'm doing my best, guv'nor."

"Blast you, Jonny Quest!" A shot rang out, and a bullet whizzed past Jonny's ear. It ricocheted off a bulkhead and crashed into some lights.

A wheezing alarm began to sound.

However, before Hyde-Pierce could get off another shot, Jonny was through the hatchway. Jessie pulled him out, and they sprawled together on the top of the vessel.

"Stand back," said Jessie. "I'm going to try something!" She stood up, holding Hyde-Pierce's radio control device. It was a struggle to keep her balance, because the whole vessel seemed to be shaking even harder than before.

Is the ship going to submerge back into the lake's deep mud once again? was Jonny's thought. He got up himself and turned around. "Look!"

The lights around the hatchway were going nuts, and the metal hatch was closing.

"Blimey!" called a voice. "Don't leave me in here with this loony!"

"Higgins, get out of my way!" Hyde-Pierce's voice commanded. "I get to climb the ladder first. I'm the scientist here—oof!"

There was the sound of a struggle, and then that of two bodies hitting the floor again.

The hatchway sealed.

"So much for their weapons," said Jessie. "Now I suggest that we get off this vessel before it sinks again."

Jonny needed no further encouragement, and both of them scurried off the alien spaceship. When they reached the shore, they didn't stop to watch but hurried up the beach and toward the jungle.

The air was hot and ragged in Jonny's lungs as he ran. When he felt they had gone far enough to be safe, he turned and looked back to see what was happening. Jessie turned back briefly, too, and Jonny could see her eyes widen.

"Oh, no! We'd better not stop here!" she yelled. "Keep running!"

Jonny felt a tremendous rumble in the ground and started running again, pulling Jessie along as well. As he ran he kept looking back at the amazing sight behind them.

The spaceship in the lake was not only shaking now. It was starting to rise, apparently lifted by an immensely powerful force. Gusts of flame jetted from the sides of the ship, making it look as though it were on fire.

Jonny ran even harder.

When they came to a rise a safe distance away, they took cover behind a large fallen log and watched the spectacle unfolding down by the lake.

The spaceship was much larger than it had seemed in the lake. It was knobby and oblong and clothed in a fierce, shuddering light.

"It's taking off!" said Jessie. "What in the world happened?"

"I don't know," said Jonny. "I must have helped it fix itself."

The alien spaceship hung in midair for a few seconds . . . and then, with a speed that stunned Jonny, it just took off, punching a hole in the clouds.

"Looks like it's going home now," said Jonny.

"Not with the best of Earth's emissaries, either," said Jessie ruefully.

They gazed up with wonder for a moment.

"What happened up there on top of the ship?" Jonny finally asked.

"When the ship started shaking," said Jessie, "Doodle turned his back on me and leaned over the hatch to see what was happening. Big mistake! I booted him."

"Good work." Jonny looked up. The ship was already long gone. "Too bad we can't get a better look at that thing now, though."

"At least we solved the mystery," said Jessie.

"And we rid the world of a couple of real pains," said Jonny. "I'd say that two out of three isn't bad—also considering the fact that our lives were at stake."

A voice behind them cried, "Hello! Hello! Are you all right down there?" An excited woof followed the words.

It was Kailish and Bandit.

"Yes, we're fine, thanks!" Jonny replied.

"I encountered your pet on the way down here, and he led the way. An excellent dog." Their guide looked up at the sky. "Amazing, what just happened here. A startling sight indeed. And it has all been recorded automatically on your equipment. Whatever happened?"

"All in good time, Kailish. Right now we've got to figure out how to get back to civilization," said Jonny. "There's a helicopter down there we can use. But first we need to get the guy who can pilot it."

"Dad!" said Jessie.

"That's right. Race Bannon, if he's up to it. And we have to get the others, too—my father and Hadji. They're back in the Forbidden City of Luxor."

"Only it doesn't seem so forbidden anymore," said Jessie.

Jonny looked up at the soft glow of the moon, which heightened the shadows around the ruined buildings of Luxor.

"Well, I don't know about that," said Jonny. "Oh, and Kailish . . . "

"Yes, Jonny?"

"How do tigers feel about helicopter rides?"

22

"WHAT DID I TELL YOU?" SAID HADJI, STRETCHED OUT IN A lounge chair by the hotel's pool. "My people know how to treat heroes, do they not?"

"I'll say!" said Jonny Quest. He lifted the tall, cool glass to his lips and sipped.

Malted milk!

They'd actually figured out how to make a malted for him!

And that wasn't all. In this private area near the hotel's pool there stood a whole spread of appetizing dishes. Not only Indian food, either, but grilled cheese sandwiches and french fries and everything that Jonny and his friends craved—even a mushroom pizza.

"Ah, this is the life," said Jessie, pulling herself out of the water. She grabbed a towel and started mopping her face. "Anybody seen my suntan lotion? I think I need another glob."

Kailish picked up a tube of the stuff and handed it to her. "I am doing the best I can to make up for your troubles here," he told the three teenagers. "I feel that if my government had supported you more, we would have had a real prize."

"Instead of a *sur*prise," said Hadji. He was working on his laptop, which had been recovered from Hyde-Pierce's rented van. "Well, at least we've got a lot of data, thanks to Kailish and our equipment. And we solved the mystery."

"And we helped launch men to the stars!" put in Jessie with a laugh.

"Poor stars," said Jonny. "Well, we can't think about that now. It's out of our hands."

"So it was Hyde-Pierce's plan to sell that ship and its secrets to the highest international bidder?" said Jessie.

"That's the way I figure it," said Jonny. He got up and stretched. "Wow. I can't take too much relaxation. I just can't get the hang of it. . . ." He went over to where Hadji was working. "Hope they didn't mess up the data on our computers too much, Hadj."

"It is very hard to say, Jonny. However, I am examining the communications section now, and—"

"Dad! Race!" Jonny cried as he saw his father and Jessie's father strolling into the pool area. "Did you find out anything else?"

Dr. Quest sucked on his pipe, frowning. He shook his head. "Nothing about the alien spaceship, I'm afraid."

Race sat down on a lounge chair. He looked tired but healthy. "Plenty about the operations of a couple of English hooligans, though. I'd say we have enough to put them away for a long time."

"If they were still on Earth, that is." Dr. Quest looked up to the sky. "I wonder what extraterrestrials are going to make of those two."

"Not exactly prime representatives of Earth," said Race. "But what can we do about it now?"

As soon as they'd recovered from the drugs that Hyde-Pierce had forced them to take and had some rest, Dr. Quest and Race had been examined by local medical doctors and determined to be in good shape. They'd told Jonny and the others how they'd been captured, explaining that their car crash had rendered them unconscious, enabling Hyde-Pierce and Doodle to take them easily. However, Bandit had fortunately scampered off to find the other members of the Quest Team.

"We got some interesting information from the readings that you and Kailish were able to take," said Dr. Quest. "However, we'll have to process that when we get back to QuestWorld." He put his hand on Jonny's shoulder. "Right now I just want to tell you—all of you, including Kailish—how proud of you I am. You all handled yourself very well in what was a crisis situation."

Bandit looked up from a bowl of food and barked.

Race laughed. "You too, Bandit. Especially you, from what I hear."

Bandit woofed, then woofed twice more. He scampered off to the other side of the pool and through the double doors into the hotel.

"Where's Bandit going?" said Jessie.

"I wouldn't worry," said Kailish. "That dog seems to

have a remarkable sense of direction. I think he'll find his way back. But Dr. Quest, I must ask you some questions. With all the data you've been able to analyze so far, what is your theory about the alien spacecraft?"

"I think that Jonny's surmises are probably more or less correct," said Dr. Quest. "Obviously the craft visited this area thousands—perhaps tens of thousands—of years ago. There was an accident, and its passengers died. Perhaps the ship's systems were on some sort of timer, and it buried itself in the lake bed. Every few hundred years or so, it would emerge for a period of time and send out a beacon to its fellows. However, Jonny was able to jump-start it . . . and presumably it headed back home."

"And now maybe we'll be getting more visits from extraterrestrials," Race said softly.

"That's hard to say. I, for one, welcome that possibility." Dr. Quest looked up toward the sky. "I *burn* with curiosity about what's up there." He turned to Jonny. "I'm so proud that you're one of the first human beings to have set foot in an alien spaceship, son."

"Thanks, Dad. It had some scary moments, but it was a real charge," said Jonny.

Barking sounded from the porch beyond. Bandit bounded out of the colorfully tiled terrace, yapping furiously.

"What's Bandit all exercised about?" said Jessie.

The answer emerged from the shadows. Running toward them was a tiger! Its eyes were bright, and it roared as it approached.

"Dr. Quest, watch out!" said Race, stepping between the danger and the Quest Team.

"Race, don't you recognize our friend?" chuckled Dr. Quest.

"It's Mrs. Thatcher!" said Jonny. His heart had speeded up at the sight of the beast, but now it was settling down.

"I requested that the owner bring her over today," said Dr. Quest. "But she seems to have slipped her leash."

The tiger came directly over to Jessie to be petted.

"It's purring!" said Jessie.

Bandit yipped excitedly.

"Bandit wants us to thank Mrs. Thatcher as well," said Hadji.

"Yes. I dare say Mrs. Thatcher is very happy to be away from those scalawags Hyde-Pierce and Doodle," said Dr. Quest.

Jonny stepped over and stroked the tiger's soft, beautiful fur. He wondered if aliens from other planets had any creature so beautiful or noble. But then, maybe aliens from other planets *looked* like Mrs. Thatcher!

Finding that out, though, would be another adventure—one that Jonny Quest was looking forward to!

SCIENTIFIC AFTERWORD

TIGERS ARE NOT ONLY TERRIFYING—THEY'RE BEAUTIFUL. MORE than any other animal, they stand for the raw power of the jungle.

Tigers earn their air of mystery by prowling mostly at night. They like the wet reeds and brush of river banks and dense jungle. They attack in a rush, at speeds of twenty miles per hour—but only for short sprints. Wild animals are their usual meals, but if domestic animals are around, those, too, go on the menu. Some favorites are goats, sheep, cattle, and horses. A tiger with a taste for cattle needs a fresh cow every five days, so a tiger can kill sixty or seventy in a year. They kill with their enormous claws and powerful jaws. Males are the largest, weighing up to five hundred pounds (230 kilograms). The largest are ten feet long (three meters), including the three-foot (one meter) tail.

The horrifying sight of a big tiger bearing down upon you is common in India, where tigers kill up to several hundred people in a year. Usually tigers turn to a people-only menu if they have injured claws, broken teeth, an injury, or are simply old. These make it hard to catch faster prey, and humans are notoriously slow. Even young tigers may hunt humans if they are hurt from gunshot wounds or have porcupine quills stuck in them. One hungry tiger killed 127 people in a year before being hunted down itself.

India's tigers are the best known—the Royal Bengal. Smart Bengals never attack elephants, and only rarely bears or large buffalo. These animals can beat off tigers and even kill them. Tiger coloring helps them hunt, too. They have a light tinge of yellow on their bellies and deep yellow or orange on their backs. Black stripes swirl over this, with black rings on their tails. These provide excellent camouflage when tigers lie in dry grass or among reeds. They make great hunters because, unlike their fellow cats, they swim and can cross rivers in search of prey. They do not like to climb trees, like domestic cats, but they will in a flood.

All tigers are closely related, and share the same scientific name, "Leo tigris." This is why Leo is a common name for both tigers and lions. In fact, lions differ from tigers only in the coloring of their coats and because tigers do not have manes. Tigers and lions can even interbreed.

Once tigers lived over most of Asia and Europe. The famous saber-toothed tiger, with dagger-like upper teeth, is extinct. Now tigers live only in southern Asia, and their numbers are dropping fast. Their real enemy is humans. We cut away jungle for farms, leaving shrinking areas where tigers can hunt.

Shooting tigers is illegal throughout most of the world, but the pressure of lost hunting land kills many tigers. Nations in Asia are now setting aside parks and forests for tigers, hoping to stop the decline of their population. As their numbers fall, they become more vulnerable to disease. Inherited defects can build up because there are not enough tigers to dilute the bad genes.

Many scientists, as well as other people, are struggling to preserve the tigers. Their beauty and awesome strength appeal to everyone. Watching a giant cat pace restlessly in a zoo is delightful, of course. But we will lose something extraordinary if we lose the possibility of seeing one in the jungle, where it is the most royal of cats.

Dr. Gregory Benford, Ph.D.
University of California, Irvine

The Real Adventures

JONNY QUEST™

IS BACK...
AND BETTER THAN EVER

REAL HEROES.

The hottest new show on TV is now the hottest new book series on the shelves.

REAL FANTASY.

From the polar ice caps, African plains, and Himalayan mountains to the exotic realms of virtual reality comes Jonny Quest™ and the Quest Team.™

REAL DANGER.

Join the Quest Team™ as they solve mysteries, embark on adventures, and court danger in each of these HarperPrism paperbacks.

only $3.99 each

THE DEMON OF THE DEEP
THE FORBIDDEN CITY OF LUXOR
THE PIRATES OF CYBER ISLAND (available in October)
PERIL IN THE PEAKS (available in December)